W9-AUB-536

HAUNTED HALLOWEEN STORIES

13 CHILLING READ-ALOUD TALES

By Jo-Anne Christensen

GHOST
HOUSE

Ghost House Books

© 2003 by Ghost House Books and Jo-Anne Christensen
First printed in 2003 10 9 8 7 6 5 4 3 2 1
Printed in Canada

All rights reserved. No part of this work covered by the copyrights hereon may be reproduced or used in any form or by any means—graphic, electronic or mechanical—without the prior written permission of the publishers, except for reviewers, who may quote brief passages. Any request for photocopying, recording, taping or storage on information retrieval systems of any part of this work shall be directed in writing to the publisher.

The Publisher: Ghost House Books
Distributed by Lone Pine Publishing

10145 – 81 Avenue	1808 – B Street NW, Suite 140
Edmonton, AB Canada	Auburn, WA USA
T6E 1W9	98001

Website: http://www.ghostbooks.net

National Library of Canada Cataloguing in Publication Data
Christensen, Jo-Anne
   Haunted Halloween stories: thirteen chilling read-aloud tales / Jo-Anne Christensen.
   ISBN 1-894877-34-9

   1. Ghost stories, Canadian (English)* 2. Halloween. I. Title.
BF1471.C475 2003   C813'.54   C2003-910942-9

Editorial Director: Nancy Foulds
Project Editor: Shelagh Kubish
Editorial: Shelagh Kubish, Sandra Bit, Nancy Foulds
Illustrations Coordinator: Carol Woo
Production Manager: Gene Longson
Cover Design: Gerry Dotto
Layout & Production: Lynett McKell

Photo Credits: Every effort has been made to accurately credit photographers. Any errors or omissions should be directed to the publisher for changes in future editions. The photographs in this book are reproduced with the kind permission of the following sources: Corbis: p. 56; Glenbow Archives, Calgary, Canada: p. 120 (ND-2-130); Library of Congress: p. 12 (USF34-034685-D), p. 46 (USZ62-117925); iStockphoto: p. 66 (Qwan Pham), p. 70 (Donnie Millar), p. 89 (Don Palmer), p. 96 (photographer n/a), p. 104 (Ross Dunn), p. 132 (Joey Chung), p. 149 (Jannet Serhan), p. 180 (Ole Geisselbrecht), p. 201 (Izabela Hubar).

The stories, folklore and legends in this book are based on the author's collection of sources including individuals whose experiences have led them to believe they have encountered phenomena of some kind or another. They are meant to entertain, and neither the publisher nor the author claims these stories represent fact.

We acknowledge the financial support of the Government of Canada through the Book Publishing Industry Development Program (BPIDP) for our publishing activities.

PC: P6

For my mother-in-law,
Stella—the best grandmother
I could have wished for my
children to have.

Contents

Acknowledgments

As we begin, please allow me a moment to thank the people who have supported me and assisted me throughout the creation of this book.

Shelagh Kubish of Ghost House Books has been generous with encouragement and unfailing in her editorial skills.

W. Ritchie Benedict, of Calgary, is always owed some credit for firing my imagination with his entertaining and insightful letters, as well as with the many strange and obscure stories that he takes the time to send to me.

My dear friend and fellow author, Barbara Smith, has lent me moral and professional support, on a daily basis, throughout the writing of 12 books now. I am always grateful to have her in my life.

I thank my children, Steven, Grace, William and Natalie, for keeping my life balanced and bright. I can't imagine how colorless the world would be if my sweethearts weren't in it.

Finally, as always, my greatest gratitude is reserved for my husband, Dennis. He inspires me every day of my writing life—sometimes by providing a marvelous story concept, sometimes with a well-timed word of advice. He is the most supportive partner I can imagine. I know that, without Dennis, I would not be where I am today.

Introduction

When I started writing this book, I envisioned a group of people sitting around a flickering candelabra, telling stories that were meant to terrify one another.

I wanted to be there.

All my life, I have loved a good story, *particularly* a frightening one. I remember being no more than three or four years old, propped up in bed with my mother while she read me a story that had something to do with hypnotism. It was a concept that, at the time, I found deliciously unnerving. At one point, I asked her how hypnotists put people into trances. Instead of offering a simple explanation, she chose to demonstrate. To this day, I have a vivid image in my mind of Mom looming over me, wearing her bizarre, 60s-era, rhinestone-studded, cat's-eye reading glasses, droning, *"You are getting sleepy…"* I also recall her eyes turning into those twirly circles that I always saw in cartoons, but I'm willing to entertain the possibility that that part of my memory was slightly enhanced by imagination.

"You are getting sleepy…"

I screamed—really, really loud. But I loved it. My mother knew the value of a dramatic moment. She was a great storyteller.

Some people really have a knack for spinning a yarn. Of course, there are also those who don't. People in the latter group just never seem to get to the *point*; they supply endless accounts of events in much the same way that my four-year-old daughter does ("…and then we played a game, and then we ate our snacks, and then we lined up to go to the gym, and then Mrs. Barr said, 'Don't push!' and then…"). There just tends to be no plot. But those who have the magic understand that a good story is not about events so much as it is about the way people react to them. They know that it is never about accuracy so much as it is about truth. They throw out constraint in favor of embellishment. And always, *always*—they appreciate the importance of timing.

I could listen to those people for hours.

Never are such talents more necessary than during the telling of a scary story. If you want to make people shiver, if you want to make them scream, you have to know exactly the right moment to reveal that the hook was hanging on the door handle, the calls were coming from *inside* the house, the woman in the picture had been dead for 20 years, *you are getting sleepy…*

Happily, most people do possess at least a measure of that ability. Most of us can entrance our friends with a good ghost story, given the proper atmosphere and inspiration. Sometimes, you need a thunderstorm. Or a campfire. Or a prop (may I suggest some wild, retro, cat's-eye glasses).

Or—how about a Halloween party.

There's one about to start. Strange tales will be told. You're invited to sit down and join the circle. Feel free to join in if you have a story of your own.

And don't mind me if I scream.

The Halloween Party
—The Beginning

Claire thought that she looked like a witch and Kate wholeheartedly agreed.

The problem was, she had been trying to look like a vampire.

"You know," she mumbled miserably as she tugged on her clingy black dress, "the whole sexy Vampirella thing. That's what I was going for. But, obviously, I can't pull it off."

"No, of course you can," Kate soothed. "I should have realized. I'm just totally dense about stuff—you know I am. And, anyway, you look awesome. What does it matter if people don't know exactly who you are?"

Claire thought that it was an easy thing for Kate to say. But, then, everything was easy for Kate, with her zit-repellant skin and her style-cooperative hair and her ability to charm everyone from teachers to jocks. She was a good, loyal friend, but there were times when her mere perfect presence made Claire feel more awkward and ill at ease.

Claire took a measured look at Kate in her exceptionally adorable genie costume and decided that it was one of those times. She flopped her own too-tall, too-skinny, black-crepe-clad self down on the bed and pulled out her fake fangs.

"You know what? I'm not going," she said. "I mean, it's just a stupid Halloween party. It's not like anybody actually cares whether I'm there or not."

"That's not true!" Kate protested.

"It *is* true, so why should I bother? It's like, I have to get all psyched up for this, and for what? I'd rather stay home, find some stupid old creature feature on TV and eat all the leftover candy."

"Oh, come on," begged Kate. "You might meet someone great!"

Claire rolled her eyes at the optimism that she had long considered to be her friend's most annoying quality.

"Oh, please," she said. "We're going to meet the same losers we meet every single day in the school halls."

"Something interesting might happen!"

Claire sat up and sighed.

"Kate," she said, "if there's one thing you should know by now it's that nothing interesting ever happens to me. *Ever.* So there is totally no point in my going to this party."

Ten minutes later, Claire was relaying directions from a creased, photocopied map as Kate navigated her rust-speckled hatchback through the eerily transformed Halloween streets.

"I can't believe you talked me into this," groused Claire. "Turn left at the corner."

The truth was, though, she was feeling a little better. A little less self-conscious and a little less apprehensive. For, although she hated parties, she did love the evening of October 31 and all the strange, dark atmosphere it came with. The hour was early, so the sidewalks were still crowded with children prowling for candy in their cute, cartoonish costumes. But here and there, Claire would see someone who was taller and obviously older, swathed in black, face hidden by some ghoulish mask or makeup, and she would feel a small, delicious tingle of what she always called "fun fear." She appreciated, more than the average trick-or-treater, the way people had painted plywood props to transform their front lawns into cemeteries and their verandas into fun houses, where something could leap out to terrify a person without warning. And she loved the way that, block after block, porch lights had been turned out in favor of flickering candles, grinning jack-o'-lanterns and the ghostly wash of moonlight.

As the girls followed their directions, however, the groups of costumed kids gradually disappeared. The cheerfully campy fright-night decorations vanished along with them as the streets grew hilly and winding and the houses were set an unfriendly distance away from the front street. By the time the old car had wheezed its way up the final hill, many of the homes could barely be glimpsed from their front entrances, which were invariably secured by imposing-looking gates.

"This can't be the right street," said Claire as she turned on the interior light and pored over the worn map. "We must have gone the wrong way back at the stop sign."

But Kate pulled confidently over to the curb behind a long line of other vehicles.

"No, this is right," she assured Claire. "This is the place."

Claire turned and saw massive, wrought-iron gates that had been opened wide to allow entrance. She saw gnarly, overgrown trees hugging a weed-infested stone pathway. She looked higher, above the treetops, and saw a slate gray turret outlined against the night sky. And she realized that she had seen the house before.

"Wait a minute!" she said. "This is the old—what was their name—the old Slater house! 'Slater Manor' or whatever."

"Yeah, that's right," said Kate. She got out of the car, shook her hair casually and smoothed the fabric of her harem pants. Claire climbed out of the passenger side and joined her friend on the sidewalk but seemed too entranced by the house to perform her own last-minute preening.

"What, have you been here before or something?" Kate finally asked her.

"Huh? No," Claire said as she pulled her gaze away from the dark turret window. "I mean, not inside. My grandfather drove me past here once. I just recognized it."

"Well," Kate said with a smile, "here's the scoop. Derek Handel's dad just bought it. And he's gonna tear it down and put up some high-priced condos or whatever. So Derek asked his dad if we could have the Halloween party here, because, I mean, who cares if the place gets trashed, right? And his dad said 'yes,' so we get to spend Halloween in this totally goth old mansion! How cool is *that?*"

"Yeah. Great," Claire said in a distracted way. She was staring at the turret once again as she and Kate began to make their way up the uneven cobblestone path.

The farther up the path they went, the darker it grew. The highest branches of the ancient trees laced together in a twisted canopy above them, blocking all but the odd fractured sliver of moonlight. The path twisted and turned until the front street, with its comforting lights, could no longer be seen. Claire and Kate held each other's hands tightly and followed the dim sound of the party.

"We must be getting close," said Kate when a particularly shrill laugh sliced through the murky darkness.

"Veddy close," came a gravelly voice from directly behind them. The girls jumped and shrieked in unison as each of them felt an icy hand fall upon her shoulder. When they spun around, wild-eyed, to face their attacker, they saw a tall, monstrous creature with twisted features wrapped in a swirling, black shroud. The thing began to emit a high-pitched, nasally sound and seemed to shrink in stature as it did. It took a moment for the girls to realize that the monster was collapsing in a fit of giggles.

"Oh, man! Oh, man, that was sweet!" the thing finally gasped.

"That was so adolescent," Claire said as she strode away with what dignity she had remaining.

"That was totally lame, Josh. We were *so* not scared," added Kate.

"Right!" laughed the monster. "I could tell how 'not scared' you were by the way you were peeing your pants! That was hilarious!"

The girls ignored him and kept walking. As they rounded the next corner, the path opened up into a neglected courtyard lit by a dozen grinning jack-o'-lanterns. The sound of pulsing music and excited voices became much louder. It was enough to drown out the Josh-monster's mocking cackle, but it made Claire uncomfortable in a worse way.

"It's your fault I'm here," Claire reminded Kate.

"Don't judge a party by the first idiot you meet," said Kate. "The most fascinating human being on the planet might be right behind that door."

As if on cue, the broad wooden door flew open, and a heavily made-up girl in a skin-tight jumpsuit lurched outside. Kate and Claire recognized her. She had spent an entire semester painting her nails in the back row of their English Lit class.

"Oh my God!" the girl moaned dramatically when she saw them. "I need some *air!*" Then she patted her rainbow-hued, mile-high afro wig and yanked her fake fur boa down from her shoulders, revealing the two glitter-painted bolts that were seemingly protruding from her neck. "I'm the 'Bride of Funkenstein'—get it?" she slurred conspiratorially to the girls as she teetered past them on her glossy, white platform boots.

Claire turned and looked at Kate. Kate avoided meeting her friend's eyes.

"Just try to have an open mind," she muttered to Claire as the two girls pulled open the door and let themselves into the Halloween party at Slater Manor.

Inside, the bass line of some repetitive dance tune throbbed insistently, vibrating the floorboards. There were bodies everywhere—gyrating to the rhythm of the music in the middle of the room, leaning against the walls, talking, and huddled in the darkest corners, making out. Strategically placed containers of dry ice sent up an atmospheric fog and an acrid smell that attacked Claire's nostrils the minute the door closed behind her. She and Kate worked their way across the room, guided only by the flickering candlelight from several ornate wall sconces and a pulsing green neon glow of undetermined origin.

The next room, they discovered, was blessedly less crowded and more illuminated. Dozens of orange and black tea lights had been arranged on a large table that also held bowls of pretzels and potato chips and a massive, sticky-looking punch bowl.

"Katie! Claire! Right on! I'm glad you guys slid by!"

It was Derek Handel, he of the father with the condominium plans.

"Derek! This is outrageous! What a perfect place for a Halloween bash!" said Kate. She reached out for the boy and kissed him once on each cheek. Claire was considerate enough to keep from rolling her eyes at the affected gesture.

"Yeah, thanks for the invitation, Derek," she added when it was her turn. It felt like a feeble show of gratitude, following Kate's effusiveness.

"Absolutely. Absolutely," he said. "So you guys are like, what, a totally hot genie and a...a gypsy?" he finished questioningly.

"Sure, why not," Claire answered in a flat tone. The uncomfortable lull in conversation that followed was enough to send Derek on his way.

"Okay, well, help yourselves to whatever. Catch you later," he said as he disappeared into the crowd.

"You know, you need to loosen up a bit," advised Kate once their host was out of earshot. "Why don't you have some punch?"

"*That* sewage?!" Claire said, pointing at the punch bowl with one long, black, acrylic nail. "You know that every one of these losers borrowed something from their parents' liquor cabinet and poured it in there. No thanks."

"It'll help you relax," said Kate as she poured a generous ladle-full of the swampy-colored liquid into a plastic cup.

"Are you deaf? I said 'no,'" Claire repeated as Kate held the cup out toward her.

Just then, someone across the room playfully pushed a friend who bumped into someone else, starting a chain reaction that ended with Kate being hit in the small of the back and thrust sharply forward. The drink that she was holding sailed out of the cup and splashed directly across the front of Claire's dress.

"Oh my God, I'm sorry," said Kate as she grabbed up a handful of napkins to absorb the spill. She began to wipe at Claire's costume in an effort to clean the sticky mess, but only managed to add a layer of soggy, white, shredded paper on top of it.

"Just—give me…" Claire said as she snatched the sodden, disintegrating napkins out of Kate's hand. She threw the pulpy mess down on the table and tried wiping at the front of her dress with her hands. "I need a sink," she finally said, and turned to walk away. When she sensed Kate following along behind her, she stopped and turned back.

"Look, no offense, but I'd rather go by myself," she snapped. "The only thing that sucks worse than this party is being told every five seconds how much I should be enjoying it!"

Claire saw the wounded look in Kate's eyes and knew that she would have to apologize. But she decided that she would do it later, after she had cooled down. Later, after she had wrung the sticky, boozy spill out of her dress and brushed off all the little, clinging bits of paper napkin. Later, when she could say "sorry" and mean it.

The kitchen was bleak and utilitarian, the least atmospheric room in Slater Manor, so nobody had bothered to decorate it for the party. Instead, it seemed to have been designated a storage area. The dull linoleum tile floor was covered with tubs that held ice and cold drinks, and the table and countertops were overflowing with cardboard boxes full of snacks, plastic cups and various other party necessities. A single, naked bulb set in the center of the ceiling threw a dim veil of yellow light over it all. Claire squinted and looked around. In the corner, she saw what she was looking for: a chipped porcelain sink with a goose-neck faucet.

With considerable effort, she managed to turn one of the ancient spigots. There was a low, belching sound from deep within the pipes, then a twisting trickle of rusty-looking water began to flow. Claire soaked a fresh handful of napkins and began to dab at her dress. After a few minutes, though, she sighed and turned off the tap. She felt no cleaner—only wetter and decidedly chilled from the cold water. She hugged herself tightly and leaned against the washstand, wondering what she should do next.

Going directly back into the main rooms of the house meant having to deal with Kate before she was ready to, so Claire took a look at the other two doors that led to and from the kitchen. One opened directly onto an old sun porch, which was virtually a dead end. The other, only a few steps away from the washstand where Claire stood, was a mystery. It had been left partially, invitingly, open. Claire stepped closer and gave the door a small push. Slowly, on loudly complaining hinges, it swung back to reveal a view of the shadowy, deserted back hall.

Including something that made Claire suck in her breath.

At the far end of the dark, narrow hall there was another ordinary-looking door, much like the one she had just opened. But the door at the end of the hall had no knob or latch of any kind, and three heavy planks had been nailed across it, securing it in place. It was still a door, but one that would take some serious effort to open.

Claire approached it cautiously.

"Oh, my God," she whispered to herself. "This must be the…"

She reached out and lightly touched it then, barely brushing her fingertips against the dark wood veneer that was drying and splintering from years of neglect. As she did, she was jolted with a zap of electricity that sent her crashing to the floor. She landed hard on her tailbone and felt an angry flash of pain when the back of her skull glanced off an old radiator. For a few moments, the world became gray and fuzzy.

"Can I help you up?"

When Claire opened her eyes, she saw an unfamiliar young man smiling down at her. She took a deep breath, decided that she was probably fit to stand and accepted his hand.

"Yeah, ouch," she said, as she rose to her feet. "I think I was just the victim of the most major static build up in the history of the world. Kinda weird, but these old houses are all death traps, right? All lead paint and asbestos tiles and boilers that are always on the verge of exploding. It's like, one wrong move, and you're toast." She looked at the young man then, who was smiling at her in a bemused fashion, and realized that she had been nervously rambling. "I'm Claire," she finished, sheepishly. "Thanks for helping me up."

"I'm Charles," the young man said, "and it was my pleasure."

Claire looked at her new friend appraisingly. He was wearing a soldier's costume—nothing that obscured his features—and she was certain that she hadn't met him before.

"You don't go to Brookside High," she said.

"No. I don't," he admitted.

"So, what, are you here with someone?"

"I guess you could say that."

Claire was surprised to feel a little pang of disappointment. She tended to be levelheaded where boys were concerned; she didn't fall in and out of love five times a day, as Kate did, but there was something about Charles that was different and instantly appealing to her. It was depressing to know that he had come with another girl.

"Oh, well, then, you'd better get back..." she began, but Charles interrupted her.

"No, I meant I'm here with *you*, now," he said, and Claire's heart lifted.

"Are you sure you want to be?" she teased. "I mean, my dress totally reeks of 'Mystery Punch' and I've been known to collapse at the slightest little static zap. Maybe you'd rather be back there, where people are having fun." She lifted her eyebrows in the direction of the muted voices and insistent, pulsing music.

Charles shook his head and wrinkled his nose.

"I prefer the quiet," he said. "And, besides," he added as he stepped back to survey her costume appreciatively, "I rarely get to spend time with a..."

Witch...gypsy...undertaker... Claire finished in her head.

But "...vampiress," was what he said. Claire felt a small lump of pure, pathetic gratitude form in her throat.

"Really," she said when she found her voice. "Well, now's your chance." Then she tucked her arm into Charles', and they went searching for a quiet place to talk.

The second floor of the huge, old house was beginning to catch the overflow from the party below. There were little groups of people sitting here and there on the floor of the broad hallway, talking and laughing. A couple of the rooms had clearly turned into "make-out zones," and one other was filled with a sweet-smelling haze that Claire often encountered in the girls' washroom at school. Upon her fourth try, however, she opened a door and smiled.

"Empty," she pronounced. "We can hang out in here."

Charles followed her into what might have been a study at one time. Claire pulled the chain of a dusty lamp with a fringed shade. Its dim light revealed a shabby selection of musty, overstuffed furniture and walls lined with floor-to-ceiling shelves of books. A cold, stone fireplace sat at one end of the room. A stuffed, glassy-eyed deer's head presided over it.

"I don't think he's having a good time either," said Claire, pointing to the moth-eaten, mounted animal.

"Could be worse," shrugged Charles. "He could be stuck downstairs, listening to all that noise."

Claire smiled but eyed Charles suspiciously as he wandered around the room, running his hands over the furnishings and ornaments. She agreed that the party was noisy and unpleasant, but she had to be somewhat wary of anyone who was as much of a misfit as she herself was.

"Okay, you're not a party animal," she said. "So why'd you come tonight?"

Charles stopped his meandering, took a deep breath and looked around the room.

"I don't know," he said. "I just like to come here sometimes. I can't help it."

"So you know this place?" Claire felt the tiny hairs on the nape of her neck rise to attention.

"Very well," Charles nodded.

"You know that they're tearing it down?"

Charles turned to Claire with a shocked expression.

"No! I knew nothing of the kind!" he said.

"Well, they are," she said. "I think it's too bad, but, like they care what *I* think. Even most of the people who are here tonight just came because they can trash the house without getting into trouble, you know?"

Claire's observation was underscored by the sound of glass breaking in the room below them. The two new friends winced simultaneously and then smiled.

"So it would seem," Charles said.

There was a moment's silence between them then, but it was an easy sort of silence. Claire liked Charles. She felt comfortable with him.

"Do you want to know something really interesting about this place?" she finally said.

Charles nodded.

"Sure. What?" he asked.

Claire took a deep breath.

"Okay—that door downstairs," she said. "The one in the back hall, where I…" she rolled her eyes "…fell down in such a glamorous fashion. Well, it's been bolted shut for something like half a century."

Charles' eyes widened and his jaw dropped a little. Claire felt the delicious satisfaction of having shared a truly intriguing secret.

"That long?" he said.

Claire nodded.

"Mmm-hmm. There's a stairway behind it that leads to the attic. But no one goes up there. Well, obviously."

Charles pressed his fingers against his temples and turned away from Claire. He kept his back to her for several seconds and she began to worry that she had disappointed him by being a gossip. When he finally did turn around, she could see that his face had changed somehow—but not toward her. Instead, he smiled and held out his hand.

"Come here," he said. "If this house is coming down, then I should first show you some things." Charles led Claire over to the bookshelves. He traced his fingers along the spines of the books as he quickly scanned the titles.

"Hardly anybody knows this," he said, "but there's a book in here that was personally autographed by—here it is." He grabbed a thin volume from a shelf above Claire's head and pulled it down. He opened the book to its title page and showed her.

"Rudyard Kipling," he said proudly. "Look, it's dated 1934. Two years before he died."

Claire took the book and gently touched the scrawl of ink on its brittle page. But before she could comment or question Charles, he was pulling her away, showing her something else.

"Over here," he said, pulling her along by the arm, "there's a bit of wainscoting with a false panel in the center. If you push on it just so…" Charles pressed gently against the top corner of the panel until it released and opened inward. "Look at that. A genuine secret hiding place!"

"Oh, my God!" squealed Claire, as she reached tentatively into the dusty alcove. "This is like stuff out of a *movie!*"

"Now come to the window," Charles said. "I'll show you another thing that most people aren't aware of."

Claire wiped her fingers on her skirt, placed the book carefully back on the shelf and followed Charles to a broad window that overlooked the front grounds. He had a faraway look in his eyes, and Claire stood patiently beside him for several moments before he began to speak.

"Do you remember how it used to be, when people with estates had their own family cemeteries?" he asked dreamily.

Claire shivered a little.

"Well, I've heard of it," she said. "Kind of creepy, if you ask me."

"Maybe," shrugged Charles, "but in a lot of families, it was tradition. It was tradition in the Slater family, but when Henry Slater married and built this house, that sort of thing wasn't allowed anymore. So he created his own sort of memorial."

"How?" asked Claire, who had decided to make herself comfortable on the cushioned window seat. But before Charles answered, her comfort was disrupted by a terrible thought.

"God, they're not in this house!" she said, jumping up and wiping at her dress as though she had been sitting on something contaminated and vile. "The bodies aren't in this house, are they?!"

Charles, who had been in such a serious mood, nearly doubled over with laughter.

"No," he finally gasped as he wiped at his streaming eyes. "Don't worry, there are no proverbial skeletons in the closet! I just wanted to point out—over there." He turned back to the window and pointed toward the tangle of trees near the front gate. "You can't really see it too well from here, but there used to be a garden off to that side, by the entrance. It's all overgrown now, but there are some marble memorial statues there. One for every Slater who died in this house."

Claire let her breath out in a relieved rush and plopped back down on the window seat. She looked up at Charles, whose eyes were still twinkling with humor, and felt an embarrassed flush creep across her cheeks.

"How do you know all this anyway?" she asked.

"I used to live here," said Charles.

Claire smacked her palm against her forehead.

"Of course! Duh! I should have known." She shook her head as if in wonder at her own stupidity.

Charles sat down beside Claire and put his hand on her shoulder.

"How *could* you have known?" he asked gently. "And, anyway, what fun would life be if we went around knowing everything? There'd be no mystery."

His sincerity was disarming. Claire realized that, at that moment, she could ask Charles a question and not worry about whether or not it sounded ridiculous.

"Listen," she said, looking into his dark eyes, "if you lived here, maybe you can tell me something. Did anything strange ever happen to you here?"

"Strange?"

Claire took a deep breath.

"Yeah. You know, like…Well, I heard that this place is haunted. I wish I could believe the person who told me. But that's totally idiotic, right? It has to be just stories."

Charles looked at Claire for what seemed to be a long time. Finally, he raised his eyebrows and shrugged.

"There's more to this world than we know," he said simply.

Claire might have pressed him for a more specific response, but the door to the study burst open then, and a swarm of costumed teens invaded the quiet space. They were led by Kate, who was lighting their way with the ornate old candelabrum that she held aloft.

"Okay, break it up, love-birds!" she cooed at Claire and Charles. "Sorry to intrude, but this has just officially become 'Ghost Story Central.'"

"Yeah!" growled a boy in a martial arts get-up. "We need room to spin our tales of ter*rah!*"

"You know, we were here first," Claire complained weakly as she watched people settling into the threadbare chairs and sofas.

"Sorry," said one girl, "but this is the best room for storytelling. And this *is* the best ghost story night of the year."

Someone who was dressed like a martian switched off the fringed lamp, leaving only the flickering candles to light the room. Cushions were thrown to the floor to provide extra seating. Furniture was moved this way and that until everyone had been drawn into a large circle. People began to wiggle down into their seats, making themselves comfortable for the duration. There was a palpable air of expectancy.

Claire turned to Charles.

"Maybe we should take off," she whispered to him. "We sort of lost our quiet place."

But Charles was eyeing the group with interest.

"No," he said, quietly. "Let's stay. I like a good story."

Claire took one look at Charles as he sat, looking handsome and pale in the soft moonlight that streamed through the glass, and knew that she wasn't going to leave without him. So she settled comfortably into the window seat beside him, near the group but separate from it, and listened as a red-haired girl in a tutu offered up the first tale.

"You guys remember my big sister, right?" the girl began. "Well she told me one of the creepiest things about where she works…"

And so the stories began…

"My sister's a nurse at Saint Joseph's Hospital. There are all kinds of stories there about this certain weird guy that the staff sees every so often. Nobody's ever talked to him; nobody knows who he is. But whenever he shows up, it's like an omen or something. They know somebody's gonna die..."

Grim

Calvin's leg was hurting like hell, but that wasn't what woke him up. It was the television. Someone had turned the volume on the TV up to a thunderous roar. It wasn't Calvin's fault; he'd been taking a nice little drug-induced nap—but he knew he'd get blamed for it just the same. The night-shift nurse had it in for him.

He willed his groggy eyes to open but couldn't quite make them focus. The painkillers that kept life bearable also made every journey from dreamland to consciousness a long, arduous one. It always felt as though he was struggling to rise from a deep pool of quicksand.

The tinny laugh track blasted out of the TV again. It had to be after midnight; it was way too late for that kind of disruption. Calvin started to pat the bedcovers, looking for the remote. He thought that he might have hit the power button while he was sleeping. Not that he moved around that much in his sleep. Not with his leg studded with pins and suspended in the contraption of ropes and pulleys that he had come to think of as "The Pain-olator 2000." There were days when it was nothing short of a torture device, but it was better than losing part of his leg, which had been a distinct possibility in the early days after he had skied directly into the tree.

Calvin's leg had been more than broken. It had been shattered. The bone was reduced to something like "pebbles in a skin pouch," his doctor was fond of saying. His doctor was a cheery sort, brimming with such colorful analogies. He was fond of telling Calvin what a good job he had done of destroying his leg.

"Well done," he would say, with a wink. "I couldn't have done a more thorough job of it myself."

The night nurse—the one named Karla who always took her time delivering his meds during the long, often pain-racked hours between 11 PM and breakfast—held a different opinion.

"You stupid show-off kids and your bloody extreme sports," she often hissed at him. "It's all fine for you. I'm the one who has to empty your bedpan for weeks on end."

Calvin knew there was no point in arguing with her. She had simply decided to hate him. And now she was going to come in and kick his groggy butt because an *I Love Lucy* rerun was screaming out of the TV.

The remote wasn't on the bed. He hoped to God that he hadn't knocked it onto the floor; if he had, that meant calling Nurse Nightmare to come in and turn the TV off for him, which would result in an immeasurable amount of misery.

Maybe I left it on the nightstand, he thought, although he knew that wasn't too likely. It was hard for him to reach the little table that sat between the two beds. It required twisting his body ever so slightly, an action that sent a hot poker of pain from his hip to his toes. Still, it would be worth it if he found the remote and didn't have to ring the dreaded call button.

Calvin pushed himself up, just a little, on his elbow. He turned gingerly in the direction of the nightstand. And he saw then that he had a visitor.

He was a short guy and thickset. It was easy to see that even though he was sitting down, tipped comfortably back on what Calvin always thought of as "the guest chair." He was a maintenance man of some sort, judging by his utility-gray coveralls and steel-toed boots. And from Calvin's teenaged perspective, he appeared to be old—in his 40s, easily. There were deep-set crow's-feet around his eyes and a bit of a jowl had begun to soften his jawline. The guy's hair had a little salt-and-pepper effect beginning to show and it was thinning visibly on top. It was on the longish side, though, and he had slicked it into a little ponytail at the back. The ponytail didn't fit the rest of the picture. A brush cut would have seemed more appropriate.

As Calvin was sizing up the stranger, Lucy let out a loud "Waaaaaaaaaaah!" The guy threw his head back and howled with laughter. He turned to Calvin then and spoke.

"I love this broad!" he gasped in a raspy, two-pack-a-day voice. "She cracks me up! I told her that, too. She died, back in '89."

Calvin nodded vaguely. He wondered if the stranger was visiting his roommate, the old man who had occupied the other bed in the room for the past week. The curtain was drawn back, so Calvin snuck a look at him. He was still unconscious, still hooked up to a bevy of machines that were apparently working in place of most of his vital organs. Just the same as he had been ever since he came in. The guy wasn't really up for company, and he never had any during the day, let alone in the middle of the night. Calvin remembered then that the hospital didn't even allow visitors past 8 PM.

"I don't think you're supposed to be here right now," he said timidly to the man in the coveralls.

The guy was laughing again, bent over, holding his gut. He brought both hands up to wipe at his streaming eyes and Calvin saw a cheap, fat cigar smoldering between two of his fingers.

"You'd better put that out," he said a bit more forcefully. His leg was really starting up now, and he wouldn't get another pill for at least two hours. He might have slept right through the pain had it not been for Lucy's Biggest Fan. The sleep cobwebs were clearing away and Calvin was starting to get annoyed. Not that the blue-collar dude was likely to care. Not about some zit-faced kid who couldn't even get out of bed to take a leak.

"Take it easy, kid," the guy said in a patronizing tone that confirmed Calvin's expectations. "I'm just on a break here. Ten minutes before my next collection. Thought I'd see what was on the ol' tube. Glad I did. Man, that Lucy!" He started to chuckle at the mere memory of the last gag as he scratched at the dark shadow of stubble on his cheeks.

Calvin couldn't believe that someone could be so dense.

"This is a hospital!" he said. "There's no smoking allowed!"

That cracked the guy up nearly as much as Lucy did.

"Like anybody's gonna complain!" he wheezed. He turned to the old man on the respirator. "You, buddy? You gonna complain?" He turned back to Calvin. "How 'bout you, junior? Gonna file a grievance?"

Calvin thought that he would. He hated to call in the wretched night nurse, but someone had to get rid of the guy. The call button was always pinned to the front of Calvin's hospital gown, for easy access, and when the guy turned his attention back to the TV, Calvin pushed it to summon help.

There was no response. Calvin pictured the evil Nurse Karla deliberately ignoring his call as she devoured the salacious contents of some trashy tabloid magazine. He buzzed again. Still no answer. This time, he imagined her peering into a compact, touching up her harsh makeup or examining the dark roots of her brassy, overly processed hair. He had no proof that she so purposely neglected him, but he would have bet money on it just the same.

A commercial for some miracle juicer came on, and the guy in the guest chair started to stretch. He groaned loudly as he cracked his spine to first the right and then the left.

"My achin' back," he said. "I been run off my feet today. Flu epidemic, hey? Makes for a busy couple of weeks. All day yesterday I spent at the old folks home over on Grove Avenue. All day!"

Calvin was still mad; his leg still hurt and he still wanted the guy gone. But he was mildly curious, too.

"What do you do, exactly?" he asked.

The guy stopped in mid-stretch and tipped him a knowing wink.

"You know," he said. "It's like, uh, 'ultimate waste management.' I collect the trash and let God sort it out."

"Are you from the morgue?" whispered Calvin. He felt a small chill run down his spine as he said the words.

The guy gave a little snort of disgust.

"Do I look like one of those bureaucrats?" he sneered. "I mean, I'm in the business, but I work at a different level entirely. I don't slow down to fill out any forms in triplicate, if you know what I mean."

Calvin had no idea what the guy meant, but he was getting nervous. And it wasn't just about the TV now or the possibility that the nurse was going to come in and give him hell for something. Calvin had begun to look anxiously at his roommate.

"Did he die?" he asked in a low, nervous tone. "Because if he did, just get him out of here. I don't wanna be stuck in here with a dead guy."

"Relax," said the stranger as he blew out a gray cloud of noxious smoke. "Nobody's dead, yet."

"What do you mean 'yet?'" Calvin pushed the call button again, very discreetly.

"I mean, I'm early," said the guy. The commercials were nearly over and his eyes were trained on the television again. "Thought I might as well get here ahead of schedule and take my break while I waited."

Calvin stared at the stranger in disbelief.

"But how do you know?" he said. "How do you know that there's gonna be a body?"

Lucy was back on the screen then, saying something funny and sweet to Ricky to wrap up the show. The guy was watching intently and missed Calvin's question.

"Huh?" he said. "What's that?" He kept his eyes on the television.

Instead of repeating himself, Calvin bluntly asked, "Who are you?"

The guy did turn to look at him then. He looked amused, maybe even a little surprised that he hadn't been recognized.

"I'm the Reaper, kid," he said with a chuckle. "Call me Grim."

Then he turned back to the television, and Calvin started pushing the call button like mad because he did not want to be alone with a crazy person any more than he wanted to be alone with a dead body.

"Don't bother," said the stranger as he watched the credits roll by. "Those things don't work when I'm around. Phones, panic buttons—none of that stuff makes a difference to me. When I'm scheduled to be someplace, nothing's gonna change it."

"Nurse!" Calvin screamed. "Somebody!" He was no longer worried about the level of noise. And, for the first time since he had arrived, he *wanted* the horrible nurse to make an appearance. Because somebody had forgotten to do a bed count on the psych ward, and he was getting more freaked out by the minute...

The lunatic started to laugh.

"Kid, they can't *hear* you," he said. "It's like we're in a bubble. Sort of suspended above reality, you know?"

There were footsteps in the hall outside.

"Help! Help me! In here!" Calvin screamed. The footsteps continued past the door and grew increasingly distant. Whoever it had been had not even paused.

The man who said he was the Grim Reaper looked at Calvin as if to say "I told you so" and shrugged.

"No one ever believes me," he sighed. He flicked his hand in the direction of the television then, and the screen went black.

Calvin watched this and saw, finally, where the remote control was. It was on the other side of the room, easily a half-dozen paces away.

"How did you do that?" he whispered.

"Break's over!" announced the Grim Reaper, and he slapped his hands on his knees with jolly enthusiasm and stood up.

Calvin felt sorry for the old man. At least he was sure that by morning, he would feel sorry for him. He might even feel a little guilty for not having done more to help. But there was nothing that he *could* do, really, and the sight of the Reaper rising to his feet, eagerly rubbing his thick hands together, was more than he could bear. If he had to witness something so terrible, he wanted to have the experience done with.

"Just go!" he begged. "If you've gotta take him, just take him and go!"

But then the Reaper looked at him slyly and said, "Who said I was here for him?" and Calvin felt his body shift from a state of fear to one of ice-cold panic.

"You can't be here for me," he said, when he was finally able to make his mouth form words. "I'm only 17."

The Reaper shook his head and chuckled. He raised his hands in humorous protest. The stogie was gone and with some detached, curious part of his mind, Calvin wondered if he had waved it away along with the TV show.

"Man, if I had a nickel for every time I heard that!" the Reaper said. "You kids think you're invincible and, lemme tell ya, you're not!" He jabbed one stubby finger in Calvin's direction for emphasis.

"'Course," he admitted with a shrug, "everybody figures they got some good reason why they can't go." The Reaper adopted a lilting falsetto tone as he began to recall his victims. " 'I just got married!' " he mimicked. " 'I never touch red meat!' "

His face lit up at a particular memory.

"Oh! Hey!" he said. "You wanna hear my favorite one this week? Guy says to me, 'I can't die! I just bought a lottery ticket!' *A lottery ticket!*" The Reaper threw his head back and had a good laugh. It was obvious that the hapless lottery-ticket owner cracked him up as much as Lucy, who had been complimented on her comedic skills when she died in '89.

"Okay, I get your point," said Calvin, "I'm not immortal. But I *do* only have a broken leg."

"Yeah, but blood clots are a funny thing, though, aren't they?"

Calvin had heard about blood clots. He vaguely remembered stories about people who had suffered some minor injury and then dropped suddenly, unexpectedly dead when a rogue clot nailed their hearts or their brains. He began to hyperventilate.

The Reaper looked at him with pity.

"Look, kid," he said, "I didn't say I was here for you, either. I just hate it when people make assumptions, ya know?"

"I can't…stand…this," Calvin gasped as he struggled to get his breathing under control. "Tell me who you're… taking." Hyperventilating was making him worry about the state of his lungs. What would happen if a big, deadly blood clot hit a guy in the lung?

The Reaper tilted his head a little and arched his eyebrows. A small smile touched his lips.

"Tell you what," he said. "I'm in the mood for a little game. I'm gonna be sporting here and let you convince me that it shouldn't be you."

"You can decide that?" Calvin was suspicious.

"Well," said the Reaper, "generally, I just follow orders. I get a list, you know? But I have a certain amount of— whadya call it?—'discretion.' I mean, nobody's gonna stick their big nose in, long as I fill my quota."

Calvin looked at him: the short, greasy, thick man in the standard-issue coveralls with his name—*G. Reaper*— stitched on the breast pocket. Then he thought about something his dad had said once, about how knowing the doorman could get you in to a place just as easy as knowing the manager would. And he supposed that it worked the same the other way around. When you wanted desperately to get out.

"Okay," he said. "I'll play."

The Reaper was delighted.

"Aha! That's great!" he cried. At once, he was standing at an ostentatious podium. Behind him, in place of the slowest-moving clock that Calvin had ever known, hung a huge scoreboard framed in flashing red lights. At the top, two names had been written in loopy neon letters: *Calvin* and *Benjamin*. Calvin assumed that Benjamin was the old man who was hooked up to the assortment of medical science's finest machines.

"How's he gonna play?" he asked.

The Reaper waved his hand in a dismissive motion.

"Don't worry," he said. "I'll play his side. Now," the Reaper raised his arms in the grand gesture of a game show host, "go ahead and tell me, Contestant Number One, why you should get to stay!" He lowered both his arms and his voice then and waggled a warning finger in Calvin's direction. "And don't give me any of that whiny 'I'm only 17' b.s.," he said, "'cuz it won't wash with me."

"But it's not b.s.," complained Calvin. "I've got my whole life ahead of me."

The Reaper rolled his eyes.

"Fine," he said. A bell sounded and the number *1* flashed on the scoreboard under Calvin's name. "Calvin has his whole life ahead of him. But Ben, here, has grand-children!" Another bell sounded and the scoreboard showed a tie game.

"I'm on the honor roll at school."

"Is this the best you can do?" the Reaper groused. "You kids today have no spirit." But the bell sounded despite his complaint, and the number *2* lit up beneath Calvin's name.

Calvin was encouraged and carried on out of turn.

"I want to go to college!" he said. "I want to get really drunk at a frat party! And I've got almost enough money saved up to buy my first car!"

Bing! Bing! Bing! The number read *5*.

"Hold your water, kid!" the Reaper protested. "This ain't 'sudden death overtime'—although that would be kind of appropriate, hey?" He took a moment to laugh at his own joke, then slammed the podium with his open hand to announce that he was returning to more serious matters.

"Okay. Ben here supports three different charities, out of his pension," the Reaper announced. "Plus, he volunteers at the library." The bell rang twice and Ben's number rose to 3. "He's got tickets for the theater next month, too. *Ain't Misbehavin'.* He's a big Fats Waller fan, and he's never seen it." The Reaper shook his head as if to say, *"Can you believe that?"* while the bell rang and the number changed to 4.

Calvin felt the flutter of panic in his chest. He was only leading by one.

"I've got a girlfriend," he blurted out of desperation. Immediately, he was sorry he had said it. Instead of the encouraging bell, a discordant buzzer sounded. Calvin's score dropped back down to 4.

The Reaper "tsk'd" in disappointment.

"Why would you lie to me, kid?" he said in a hurt tone. "Did you think I wouldn't know? You got no girlfriend—just some blonde chick in your chemistry class who you're lusting over. Let me give you a little insight, my friend—she's dating a junior in college and thinks your name is 'Kevin.' Now Ben, on the other hand, has a wife. She's got Alzheimer's. And if I take him—she goes into an institution; there's no gettin' away from that."

The bell rang, and Ben pulled into the lead.

"You think Blondie's gonna be that affected by your tragic demise?" asked the Reaper. He was looking serious.

He had abandoned the broad game-show-host flourishes and had stepped out from behind the podium.

"Tell me," he insisted, "will the skirt in chem class even care?"

"No." Calvin's voice was barely audible.

"So you got anything else to say to me? Or are we done here?"

Calvin said nothing. The Reaper began to turn around. He raised his arm up in the air and Calvin knew that when it came down, the game show set would be gone. He'd be going for a little ride then, and in the morning the usually cheery doctor would be making a solemn call to…

"Wait! I got one! Wait!" Calvin shouted.

The Reaper turned around, his hand still in the air.

"Oh yeah?" he said. "Well, hurry up. Time's a wastin'."

"Please don't take me," said Calvin. "I'm begging you, please, *please* don't take me now because, if you do, I swear, it will *kill* my parents."

The Reaper stopped. He stared off into space for a moment, as though he was checking some invisible data bank. Then he nodded.

"Yeah, that much is true," he said. "I got projections telling me that if I take you now, I'm back for your ma in a year or so. Tranquilizers, I think." He wrinkled his nose in distaste.

The bell rang. Calvin's score tied with Ben's at 5.

The Reaper looked at the scoreboard and sighed heavily.

"It looks like we got us one of those no-win situations here, kid," he said. "And I'm sorry, you know, but I gotta fill my quota. I gotta take someone."

There was a voice out in the hallway then, a voice that Calvin recognized. His eyes barely flicked toward the door and the wicked, ignoble thought barely flashed across his conscious mind, but neither the glance nor the thought went unnoticed. When he looked back at the Grim Reaper, he saw a devilish smile spreading across his face. The game show podium and scoreboard had vanished.

"Okay," said the Reaper. He was nodding his head thoughtfully and looking at Calvin with newfound respect. "I like you, kid, so—okay."

The Grim Reaper walked out of the room. Calvin watched him just sort of *stroll* out, like a maintenance grunt who was finished his coffee break and had to get back to work. A second later, there was a loud, metallic crash in the hallway.

In his mind's eye, Calvin imagined that the night nurse, Nurse Karla, had been carrying a tray lined with little plastic cups full of pills. He saw them spraying across the wide hallway floor like dozens of tiny marbles as the person carrying them suddenly crumpled into a prone heap of polyester uniform and disheveled, brittle hair. He thought that there would be a gaudy clown-smudge of makeup where her face had met the tile.

Every patient on the floor who was expecting medication would be getting it late, Calvin knew. According to the clock that had returned to the wall opposite his bed, his own painkiller was past due. Not that he would have known it, aside from the time. He was feeling really good; he was feeling the best he had felt since taking that wrong turn on the ski hill.

"Karla? Are you alright?" came a voice from the hall.

"Did she hit her head?" came another.

"I don't know. I just heard a crash and I found her here."

Despite the noise just outside the room, despite the overdue painkiller and despite all he had just been through, Calvin went to sleep then. He slept dreamlessly for hours until the friendly, gossipy day nurse woke him with his breakfast tray and the sad news that Nurse Karla had died suddenly during the night.

"An aneurysm or something," she speculated in a low voice as she propped him up in front of his bowl of gluey-looking oatmeal. "She was only 34. It makes you think, doesn't it? You never know when it's going to be your time." She remembered her bedside manner then and added with false brightness, "Of course, *you* don't have to worry about things like that! You're not even old enough to vote!"

"I don't think that makes any difference," Calvin said with some authority.

"Oh, poof!" said the nurse. "Don't be silly!" Then she left him to his breakfast, pulled back the curtain and walked over to the other side of the room to check on the old man.

"He's doing better," said Calvin around a mouthful of cold, limp toast. "He's gonna be okay."

The nurse flashed him a startled look.

"How did you...?" she began before she realized that Calvin was just making optimistic small talk. He couldn't possibly know what she was reading on the machines.

"You know, I think you may be right," she said instead. "Seems like everyone is doing well in here today! You'll be back on a pair of skis in no time, you'll be feeling so good!" she teased on her way out of the room.

Calvin smiled and nodded. He did feel good. And he had every reason to. For, although it may have sounded like a cliché, he did have his whole life ahead of him; it was bright and promising and only the tiniest bit tarnished by feelings of guilt.

He supposed that it was impossible to commit murder and not feel *some* guilt. But he imagined that it would be easy enough to forget, given that no one would ever suspect or accuse him and the weapon—a shameless, fleeting thought of *take her*—would never be found.

"Somebody had to go," Calvin muttered to himself as he pushed away the dirty dishes from the first breakfast he had finished since his accident. "That's a fact."

And, as anyone who has ever looked death in the eye knows, sometimes the facts can be decidedly grim.

"Do you remember that thing that happened at the Belmont Hotel last year? Well, I know this guy whose cousin was there when it happened. His name was Danny…"

Room For One More

Never in all of his 16-and-a-half years did Danny think that he'd end up being grateful for the nightmare. It had always caused him such misery. There was the lack of sleep, of course, and the anxiety. There was the way his mother gave him grief when he woke her up in the middle of the night with his screams, and the way his skin erupted in a relief map of mountainous zits after the nights he ate entire bags of cookies or potato chips to keep himself awake. No, gratitude really didn't factor into it. Not until that day at the hotel, not until after what happened there. Before that, he had seen the nightmare as a pure affliction. It was his personal cross to bear. That was *before* he found out how it ended.

For as long as Danny could remember, it had been the same.

He dreamed that he was in some kind of castle. At least, that's what it seemed to be—there were ceilings so high they could hardly be seen, and the windows were heavily draped with huge red velvet panels. There was a clanking noise that he could hear, a metallic sort of clanking, which seemed to be coming from outside. Danny would walk over to the window to investigate— no easy task, because his body had been tightly wrapped in mummy-style bandages that had gone urine-colored with age. Despite the struggle, he always managed to get to the window. And when he pulled back the curtain and looked outside, he always saw the same thing: an immense metal gate was being rolled back, allowing a horse-drawn hearse to enter the grounds. It was blacker than the night. The horses, too, were the color of coal, and their eyes burned like embers. As they drew closer to the castle, Danny could see their cargo. Coffins had been stacked like cordwood inside the hearse. With a sort of dream intuition, he knew that the coffins weren't empty; each one carried a decaying corpse. At that point, he began to back away from the window in revulsion. But before he could pull the heavy velvet draperies shut, the driver of the hearse—a beak-nosed, glittery-eyed old man—would catch his eye. He would smile at Danny in a way that sickened him and then say the terrible words.

"Room for one more!"

"That doesn't sound so bad," his friend Kevin had once said with a shrug.

"God, Danny, that's not even *scary*" had been his mother's response.

There was just no way of describing it properly in the daylight. There was no way to explain how the dread filled his chest when he saw that terrible carriage or how, when the driver smiled, Danny could sense that his long, yellow teeth were razor sharp at the tips, sharp enough to slice through human flesh. He couldn't express it, so he stopped trying. He silently suffered the nightmare, which plagued him at least twice every week, and he silently suffered the effect it had on him.

He did poorly in school. He had few friends. And he evolved into a twitchy sort of kid who was easily dismissed as high-strung. Amid the constant flow of small failures, there were the occasional momentous ones, too. Like the time he fell asleep in study hall and had a full-blown, scream-out-loud version of the dream there. Or the time he wrote a scholarship exam after a jittery, wakeful night and blew the opportunity to smithereens.

It wasn't like it had been for a college scholarship or anything. He didn't stand a chance at one of those. It had been for a summer school thing, a special activities program for teens from low-income families. It wasn't such a big deal that Danny hadn't gotten it, but, of course, his mother hadn't seen it that way.

"Well, don't think you're going to hang around here playing video games all summer," she had said. "You're going to have to work now, like the rest of the world. Margaret said that she can get you a job as a bellboy at that posh hotel of hers."

Margaret was his mother's friend. The posh hotel wasn't hers, strictly speaking; she worked there as a chambermaid, making beds and scrubbing toilets. But she had been employed there for about as long as Danny had been alive, so he guessed that she could get him a summer job. And he imagined that it wouldn't be so bad. So he showed up on the appointed day and answered all the interviewer's questions politely.

"I suppose you'll do," said the man (when Danny read about him later, in the newspaper, he found out that he had been the *Chief Concierge*, a Very Important Person). "And we're so short-handed that we haven't much choice but to offer you the position. Are you able to start immediately?"

Danny said that he was, and the man pulled out an ugly uniform, the color of faded tobacco leaves, and showed him to a room where he could change his clothes. When Danny came out, the man cast a critical eye over him.

"Awfully tight, I think. Not attractive at all." The man was looking at Danny as though it was his fault the ugly uniform with its jaunty little epaulettes didn't fit. "No, it won't do," he finally declared with a feminine flick of his hand. "We'll find something more suitable downstairs at the laundry. Please follow me."

The man walked out of the back office and began to cross the expansive hotel lobby. Danny struggled to keep up, but the uniform restricted him to tiny, mincing steps. Being more concerned about pleasing his new employer than he was about appearing ridiculous, he attempted to trot—but his arms, bound by their tight sleeves and the narrow cut of the jacket, had such a small range of motion that he feared losing his balance. So he did his best, scuttling along, and felt himself flush a deeper shade of crimson every time the concierge turned around and waved his arm in a sharply impatient gesture.

"This way! Hurry along!" he said. "The elevators are over here." He pointed to an area that was set off to one side of the lobby, beyond a dramatic gray stone archway.

There was a long bank of elegant, old-fashioned lifts. Each one had a half-moon dial above it, with an ornate curlicue of an arrow indicating which floor that particular elevator was on. Smartly uniformed operators called out the floor numbers and opened and closed the intricate, wrought-iron doors with their gloved hands. *Very posh*, Danny heard his mother's voice say in his head.

Very posh, with all of the sumptuous scarlet draperies framing the archway and the high, domed ceiling with its stained glass skylights.

Very posh. Like a castle.

And suddenly, Danny didn't feel well at all. The tingling sensation of rising gooseflesh moved across his body in waves. His chest tightened until he could take in air only in small sips. The short, fine hairs on the back of his neck crept to attention, and his stomach clenched into a small, hard knot.

"Are you coming, I said?"

The concierge was standing in a crowded elevator, looking more angry now than impatient. Danny felt waves of hostility coming off the man; he knew that he was wasting his time, causing him to be late for his next interview. Not to mention the fact that he had begun to sweat profusely in the ugly, confining, infection-yellow suit that did not belong to him. But when he tried to take a step forward, he felt rooted to the plush carpet. And when he tried to talk, his hot, dry throat could produce nothing more than a sort of clicking sound. Danny had heard people speak of being paralyzed by fear—but he had never known that it could literally happen.

The elevator operator began to close the door with his immaculate gloved hand. The rattle that it made—the hollow, metallic *clanking* of it—made Danny want to clap his hands over his ears. But he couldn't stop staring at the sight, which might have been what caused the operator to pause when the door was pulled only halfway across. He looked out at Danny from beneath raised, bushy eyebrows and spoke.

"Room for one more!" was what he said.

The man looked fine; even at that horrible moment Danny registered that the elevator operator *appeared* absolutely normal in every way. But it was a shimmering mirage sort of appearance, and Danny knew that beneath it there were wicked, glittery eyes and a thin hook of a nose and yellow, razor-edged teeth that could slip neatly through his flesh and peel it away from the bone.

"Will you *hurry!*" demanded the concierge.

"Let him catch the next one," grumbled another passenger.

The elevator operator shrugged and pulled the metal cage closed. He locked it into position with a final clang and called out, "Going down!" Danny watched the car sink slowly into the floor. The crisscross pattern of the cage framed the faces of the passengers—including the furious, purple face of the concierge—like the outlines of a dozen wooden coffins.

The hotel had been built into the side of a hill overlooking a picturesque lake. Its design was such that the lobby was on the third floor, ground level on the side of the street, where guests turned their cars over to the hustling valets and walked in the grand main entrance. The second floor was given over to rows of banquet and conference rooms, each with a spectacular view of the water. On the first floor, there was an elegant dining room and lounge. It featured a huge wall of glass doors, which opened to a lovely garden terrace that was cooled by gentle breezes off the lake. Below that was the basement, with its huge kitchen and maze of clerical offices. The sub-basement, with the mechanical rooms and laundry, was at the lowest level. Even people who had never set foot in the hotel knew these particulars by the following day. The information was necessary in that it explained the fact that after the rotting, aged cables snapped, the elevator had plummeted not one, but *four* full floors before it came to a crashing, mangled halt and killed all those who were unfortunate enough to be inside.

Danny had known that right away. He had heard their screams going all the way down.

Nothing much changed after that. Danny didn't bother looking for another summer job and his mother didn't say too much about it. He was pretty busy at first, anyway, being a minor celebrity of sorts: The Kid Who Refused To Get On The Doomed Elevator. But that died down after 10 days or so, after some crazy farmer two counties over locked his wife and kids in a pickup and purposely parked them on the railway tracks in front of a freight train. The whole thing about all the people who died in the elevator got to be old news, and things went back to normal.

Danny's nightmares even returned.

Not the one about being in the castle, not the one about the horrible, horse-drawn hearse full of corpses. That particular terror had apparently retired after serving its ghoulish purpose. But a new dream—every bit as vivid and vile—had slipped into Danny's subconscious, neatly filling the void. After the first night that he had it—when he awoke in a tangle of perspiration-soaked sheets at the foot of the bed with his fist stuffed into his mouth to stifle the screams—he was as much horrified by the knowledge that he had *had* a nightmare as he was by the nightmare itself. And the nightmare, itself, had been a corker.

In it, the bloody, crushed corpse of the Chief Concierge was advancing on him.

"Why didn't you warn me?" the man moaned quite clearly, though his lower jaw had come unhinged and had been jammed crookedly up around his ears. *"Why didn't you SAVE MY LIFE?"*

Danny had no answer, which may have been why the new nightmare plagued him almost constantly. But frequency wasn't the worst of it. When Danny lay awake in the inadequately comforting light of his bedside lamp, feeling the shadowy hollows deepening beneath his eyes, he knew what the worst of it was.

It was that he couldn't stand to imagine a time when he might find out how this one ended.

"There was this one time that my uncle had been driving all night and, just before dawn, the weirdest thing happened to him…"

The Accident Scene

When Hal thought about it later—after everything had happened—he realized that none of it would have happened had it not been for his son's birthday party. The fact that he was trying so hard to be a good father had put him on the road at that unlikely hour. The fact that the woman was doing her best to be a good mother had put her there. He thought about that sometimes when he couldn't sleep, when he would sit at the foot of his son's bed listening to the reliable whisper of his breath. But he tried not to think about it too much. When he thought about it too much, it made him feel nervous and vulnerable. It made him realize that, with a few cruel twists of fate, he could have been playing the opposite role.

"Don't worry," he had told his wife when she objected to his going away the week before the party, "I'll have this client signed, sealed and delivered by Friday morning. I'll be home by Friday night at the latest, in plenty of time to host the shindig on Saturday." But the sale took longer than he had thought it would, and then the new client insisted on being taken out for dinner. It was almost 9 PM before Hal got on the highway. He had armed himself with two thermoses of coffee and a half-dozen donuts because he knew that he would be driving all night. His wife hadn't been crazy about that either.

"I don't like you driving at night," she told him when Hal had called to say that he was leaving, "and with no sleep, to boot."

"Would you rather I miss the party?" he asked. It was Jason's sixth. They had invited 15 first-graders and a clown.

"I wish you had waited 'til next week to go out of town," she grumbled.

"But I didn't," Hal said wearily. "I couldn't. So I'll see you at breakfast."

"But what if you have an accident?" she asked.

"Oh, for God's sake—I won't," he promised. And, for the next seven hours and fifteen minutes, he didn't.

It was four o'clock in the morning by that time. Hal had been driving nonstop, guzzling his coffee and blaring the radio when he was able to find a station that he liked. But in the lonely hour before dawn, as he wound his way through a steep mountain pass, his bone-stock AM receiver was picking up nothing except a static-laden rebroadcast of a hockey game that he had already seen. So Hal turned off the noise, stretched his spine out as best he could and forced himself to blink. His eyes felt bloodshot and nearly dry from the strain of peering through the darkness at the narrow, twisting ribbon of highway, but he didn't mind. It was a small price to pay to keep his son happy.

Hal was driving cautiously, slowing his speed slightly as he approached a dangerous curve. He risked taking his eyes off the road for the briefest of moments, though—to choose between the cruller and the maple creme donut, the last two in the box—and when he looked back up, his heart nearly seized in his chest. Out of nowhere, there had appeared a dark-haired woman. She stood in the middle of the road, directly in the path of the car, waving her arms frantically above her head. The twin beams of Hal's headlights were trained on her like rifle sights.

Hal jumped on the brake pedal and nailed it down to the floorboards. The anti-lock system made its grinding, foghorn noise, but the car still wouldn't stop. There was no one in the oncoming lane, but Hal knew that if he tried to steer into it at the speed he was going, he would likely sail off the highway and into the deep gorge on the other side. Instead, he twisted the steering wheel sharply to the right. The car lurched onto the gravel shoulder. It scraped along 20 or 30 yards of steel guardrail sending up an impressive shower of sparks before it finally came to rest at the beginning of the treacherous curve.

With a shaking hand, Hal shifted the transmission into "park" and turned off the ignition. He sank back against the seat, closed his eyes and listened to the underwater sound of blood rushing past his eardrums. His pulse began to slow then, and the sweet sensation of pure relief washed over his body.

"I'm all right," Hal whispered. "Everything's okay."

Then he remembered the woman.

He was sure he hadn't hit her; he was *pretty* sure, at least. But everything had happened so fast and it had been a rough ride. Would he have noticed one more bump? Hal grappled with the buckle of his seat belt and prayed fervently that when he got out of the car, the woman would still be there.

At first, it appeared that she was not. Hal stood on the rough asphalt, breathing in the cool night air and scanning the area for some sign of her. When he saw nothing, he began to desperately examine the grill of his sedan. He wasn't sure what he was looking for; he only knew that he didn't want to find it.

"This way! Over here!"

Hal gasped and jumped back. He barked one shin hard against the post of the guardrail and had to grab a handful of crumpled front fender to keep himself from falling. The woman who had been standing in the road was now standing no more than 6 feet away from him. In the pre-dawn gloom, he hadn't seen her approaching.

"Please!" she said. "There's been a terrible accident and I need your help."

Hal could see that the woman was hurt. Her light-colored tracksuit was soaked with dark, wet patches of blood and she was holding her grotesquely crooked right arm protectively with her left. A relief map of welts and bruises had begun to rise along one side of her face, and her nose looked crooked and swollen. There was blood welling like tears in one of her pale, blue eyes.

"Oh, my…Get in," Hal said. He started to usher the woman around to the undamaged side of the car. "Get in the back," he urged. "The car's banged up a bit, but I'm sure it'll run. There's a town 15 minutes from here—I can get you to a hospital…"

But the woman was shaking her head and backing away.

"It's not me," she said. "It's my son. Come help me save my son!"

Hal looked across the road to where the woman was heading. For the first time, he noticed the neatly flattened section of guardrail. When he crossed the road, he saw a roughly cut trail leading down the steep embankment behind it and a twisted wreck of a car planted nose first in the gully below. From the road, the vehicle was completely hidden. Even at the edge of the slope, Hal had to lean over a little to get a really good view.

"My husband was driving too fast," the woman explained. There was a hitch in her voice and Hal could tell that she had started to cry. "He always drove too fast, in the dark. Now he's dead, and my little boy is trapped in his car seat. I tried to get him out, but my arm…"

"It's all right," Hal said, "It's all right." Inwardly, he kicked himself. Things were about as far from "all right" as he could imagine. "I'll get your son," he assured the woman. "You wait here. There's no sense in you walking back down there."

But the woman insisted.

"I want to help," she sobbed. "I can't just stand here. I want to be with him."

So they traveled together down the trail that the car had gouged out of the embankment. The woman kept her injured arm cradled close to her body but seemed to have no problem negotiating the steep path. She was more sure-footed than Hal, in fact, who slipped more than once in the mud and dewy grass. She reached the wreckage several seconds before he did and stood beside what remained of the front of the vehicle, waiting for Hal to arrive and open the rear passenger door.

"That door sticks sometimes," the woman instructed. "You have to lift the handle, push the door in a bit, and then pull it."

Hal did as she said and managed to yank the door open. A sour, coppery smell wafted out of the crushed vehicle. *That's the smell of death,* he thought. *Blood and death.*

"Is he still breathing?" the woman was asking anxiously. "Is my baby breathing?"

Hal peered into the back seat. There was a bit of dim morning light bleeding into the sky, enough that he could see shapes and movements. There was a small child—no more than three, he thought—strapped into a car seat in the back. He was unconscious, but Hal could see his small chest rising and falling in a regular rhythm.

"He's okay," Hal reported to the boy's mother. It was more than he could say for the two people who had been riding up front. The woman's husband—the one who had been driving too fast—had paid for his speed by becoming one with the steering column. Another person—Hal didn't care to look closely enough to see if it was a man or a woman—had been brutally crushed against the dashboard.

"It's a good thing you were riding in back with your son," Hal said to the woman. "That's what saved the two of you."

The woman nodded tersely, but it was obvious that she didn't care to hear Hal's assessment of the accident.

"Get him out," she begged. "I don't want him to wake up and see his father—that way. Please get him out of there."

She explained to Hal how to loosen the straps of the car seat's harness and unlatch the buckle. He followed her instructions, step by step, and then carefully lifted the boy out of his seat. As Hal moved him, the child began to squirm and cry.

"Oh!" said his mother, excitedly. "Oh, that's a good sign, isn't it? That's wonderful!"

She made no move to touch the boy, though, not even with her uninjured arm. Hal imagined that she was in too much pain to move very much and tried to soothe the wailing youngster himself.

"There, there," he said, patting him gently on the back. "There, there, little guy."

"His name is Joey," the woman told Hal as she started up the bank.

"You're okay, Joey," Hal said. The boy calmed down somewhat at the sound of his name. Hal was able to get a firmer grip on him and carefully started to climb back up to the road.

When he reached the top—sweating, panting and with a cramp in his arm from clutching the child—the woman was already standing by his car. She was looking anxious again, frowning and pacing back and forth. Hal wished she would stay still. The blood drenching her clothes had to be coming from somewhere, and she had to be aggravating her injuries with so much nervous activity.

"Your tires," she said as he crossed the road toward her. "Your tires on the other side of the car—they're flat. We can't drive into town that way!"

Hal held out his hand in a calming gesture.

"Don't worry," he said. "I have a cell phone. I'll call for help."

It was only 10 minutes before they could hear the siren wailing in the distance. Hal had spent the time making the woman comfortable in the back seat of his car. She had settled down, finally, and was lying limply against the upholstery. She kept talking, though, giving instructions to Hal as he paced outside the open door with her child in his arms.

"Remember what I told you," the woman said as the emergency vehicles came into view, "he's allergic to penicillin. And he likes a night-light." She had closed her pale, blue eyes and her voice was whispery and low. She sounded as though the last of her strength had run out.

Hal was relieved to see the big, white ambulance pulling up behind them. He could sense that the woman wasn't doing too well. He tried to hide his concern, though. He tried to sound encouraging.

"You'll be fine," he said. "You'll be able to take care of Joey yourself in no time!"

Two paramedics jumped out of their rig and hurried over toward the car. Hal walked over to meet them.

"This little guy was in the accident, but I think he's okay," he reported to them. Then, in a lower voice, he added, "The mother's in much worse shape."

"Where is she?" asked one of the medics.

"Over here," said Hal, and he led them back to his car.

"Where?" said one of the men again as he peered into the back seat.

Hal looked. The woman was gone.

She wasn't sitting in the car; she hadn't stepped outside and collapsed on the ground; Hal scanned the road and couldn't see her anywhere.

"She was just here!" he insisted as he handed the child over to one of the paramedics. "She was *right here!*"

A police cruiser had pulled in behind the ambulance by then. A tall, middle-aged cop was walking over toward Hal and the medics.

"Who was there?" he asked in a deep voice. "Who are we looking for here?"

Hal was struck by an idea.

"The wreck!" he said. "She's disoriented—the boy's mother—she probably went back down to the wreck! Her husband's body is there…"

"Show me where," said the cop. Hal led him across the road and, together, the two men began the slip-sliding descent into the gully.

In the pale, gray dawn, Hal could see the whole accident scene. But he couldn't see the woman. He knew that she had to be there somewhere, though. There was no place for her to hide up on the road, and she had been too weak to wander very far.

"God!" exclaimed the cop, when he reached the mangled vehicle and peered into the front seat. "People who don't wear seat belts should have to clean up one of these messes. Were these two dead when you got here?"

"Oh, yeah," said Hal. "Definitely very…" and his voice trailed off then as he glanced through the gaping hole where the windshield had been and got his first good look at the second corpse in the front passenger seat.

It was a woman. She had dark hair. She was wearing a light-colored, blood-soaked tracksuit. Most of her face was planted firmly in the remains of the pulverized dashboard, but Hal could see one of her fixed, dead eyes, staring skyward.

It was a familiar, haunting shade of pale blue.

Hal ended up telling the cop and the paramedics that he had been confused about the woman; that there had been no one else at the accident scene. He said it was pure luck that he had suffered his own little mishap at that exact location, and that the sound of the boy crying was what had drawn his attention to the wreckage of the other vehicle. Pure luck. He didn't even want to think of how long the little guy would have been trapped down there otherwise.

"How's he doing, anyway?" Hal asked the paramedic who was checking him over.

"Seems good," the man said. "We're going to observe him for a bit."

Hal nodded. Then he told the medic, "His name's Joey. And, if you ask me, it looks like he's allergic to penicillin."

The medic shot him a strange look. Hal shrugged.

"Of course, I'm only guessing," he said.

But he wasn't.

Hal missed Jason's birthday party. But he was home by that evening and grateful to be there. He told his wife most of the story; he felt that she had a right to know. But he never told anybody all of it. He was afraid, he supposed, that no one would believe him. Or that, if they did, they would think him stupid. Every time he looked back on it himself, he felt foolish for having missed the obvious thing, the first thing that he saw. The image was permanently burned into his memory. He could close his eyes at any time and see it all over again.

The woman, standing in the road, whitewashed in the harsh glare of his headlights.

Frantically waving him down—with her totally useless, horribly broken arm.

"When we lived on River Street, there was this guy next door who just suffered from the worst bad luck you could imagine. One thing after another. And he told me one time, when he was kinda drunk, that it was all because he was haunted. And you'll never guess what he said was haunting him..."

The Tip

It was only 7 AM—the breakfast rush wasn't close to being over—and the callouses on Ruth's feet were already beginning to burn. One of the coffee makers behind the long Formica counter wasn't working, and a group of college kids who had taken up a booth for more than an hour while they nursed hangovers with eggs and pancakes had left her 10 pennies in the shape of a smiley face for a tip. Customers kept asking for substitutions and special orders, oblivious to the fact that Rudy, the cook, was in a hell of a cranky mood. And then there was the guy in the rumpled tan trench coat, the one who had mumbled out his order for a decaf and a donut, who had begun to look at her in a strange way.

Ruth could handle herself. She had been a waitress for 15 hard years. But she didn't feel like dealing with a weirdo during the sort of morning she was having. So she avoided eye contact with the man and told herself that it was no big deal. He didn't look like the kind of guy who usually tipped anyway.

When he left, however, he proved her wrong. His coffee had barely been sipped, the stale donut was only picked at, but the man had neatly tucked a five-dollar bill and a quarter beneath his saucer. It was a huge gratuity for such a small order—more than generous, considering the dismissive way she had treated him—and Ruth felt her conscience prickle uncomfortably. Then she heard the cash register ring and looked up in time to see the man scurrying out through the double doors at the front of the café. He glanced back over his shoulder and jumped a little when he saw Ruth watching him. She felt even more ashamed then, for she noticed the bruise that was fading on his cheekbone and the torn pocket on his coat that flapped in the wind like a loose piece of skin.

He's had a run of bad luck, she thought and wished that she had been more kind. As the man hurried across the parking lot toward a muddy sedan with a crumpled fender, she thought that she could detect a limp, evidence of some other injury that was fading like the bruise.

Ruth grabbed the money and stuffed it into the pocket of her gingham-checked uniform. There was a slight notch on the rim of the quarter—a tiny little pie-slice that had been filed out of it—and its rough edge pricked her thumb as she put it away. It was barely a scratch, not even enough to draw blood, but Ruth felt her mood darken when it happened.

"Nothing's going my way today," she said to herself as she began to clear the table.

She deftly balanced the cup, saucer and sticky donut plate in her left hand. With her right, she reached for an empty water glass that sat on the table, nestled up to the salt and pepper shakers and the sugar packets. It was a long reach, though—"it exceeded her grasp," her prim mother would have said—and when she tried to close her fingers around the glass she clumsily sent it skidding off the table. She lunged forward, meaning to catch it before it could bounce off the padded vinyl bench and hit the floor. Ruth did grab it, but with such force that she ended up smashing the glass against the edge of the table. She stood there for a long moment, holding the dirty dishes in one hand and the jagged base of the tumbler in the other. Then she felt the heavy silence of the customers and followed their stares and saw that a large shard of glass—a perfect, spear-like piece—had imbedded itself deeply in her forearm.

She was at the hospital for hours. They stitched her and bandaged her and gave her a nice, strong painkiller. Then they released her and told her that she was free to go home. Ruth may have been free, but she had no idea how she was going to get home. Her purse was back at the restaurant, tucked away in her personal cubbyhole in the staff room. It was the last thing she had been thinking of as one of her regular customers had wrapped three of Rudy's white aprons tightly around her arm and then whisked her away to the emergency ward in the cab of his old pickup. Even if she had remembered, the purse wouldn't have seemed important at the time. But now she was stranded—without keys, cab fare, bus fare or even change to make a phone call. Ruth sighed and sat down in one of the molded plastic waiting room chairs. As she did, she felt something crinkle in her pocket.

Each of the waitresses at the restaurant had a quart-sized tip jar sitting on a low shelf behind the long, white counter. The women would shove the money that was left for them into the patch pockets of their uniforms until there was a lull that allowed them to empty it all into their personal jars. Sometimes they would be too busy to stop, and their pockets would get bulging and heavy with change. And sometimes something would happen to make them forget that they had just collected a tip. Something like a dagger of glass jutting out of your forearm could make a person forget.

Ruth reached across her body with her uninjured arm and fished her last tip out of her pocket. It was the five-dollar bill and the quarter that had been left to her by the man in the tan overcoat; $5.25—a strange amount. But, then, he had been a strange fellow. Or perhaps he had been a prescient fellow who had known that, before lunchtime, Ruth would need a quarter for a phone call.

There was a circular stand of pay phones right in front of the exit doors. Ruth supposed that it was the place where everyone who was too injured, ill or drugged to drive called to arrange a ride home. She plugged her quarter into the slot and dialed her own phone number. Her husband would be there. He was *always* at home when other people were working; Ruth often said in a cynical tone that his utter dependability was one of his few charms.

The phone rang four times and then the answering machine picked up.

"Karl?" Ruth said at the beep. "Are you screening? If you're there, please pick up."

She counted silently to 10 but held out little hope. She had overheard a nurse saying that the temperature outside had been soaring. The cool, dewy morning had turned into a scorcher of a summer day. It was the kind of day that made it easy to imagine Karl relaxing in their tiny backyard, with a beer in his hand and the kitchen radio blaring through the window.

"Useless," Ruth muttered as she hung up. Her quarter clinked into the bowels of the pay phone. That meant that she needed to get change for her five-dollar bill and think of another person to call. Still, oddly enough—she felt her mood lighten.

This is all small stuff, she thought. *It could be a lot worse.*

That was true: the doctor told her that she had suffered no tendon damage, no nerve damage, no permanent damage of any kind. She'd be all right. And when she did finally get home, she would put her feet up and watch a movie or two and make Karl order some take-out food for supper.

Ruth was starting to hum as she walked away, so she didn't hear the quarter drop back down into the change slot.

▲

Eddy was finished his morning janitorial shift; he was done pushing the big broom down the wide hospital corridors for another day. Quitting time felt good—particularly when it was an early quitting time and a jewel of a hot summer day stretched out infinitely in front of him—and there was a spring in his step as he made his way out of the building. He was singing some top 40 tune under his breath, getting most of the lyrics wrong and not caring, and pausing in front of every vending machine en route to check for abandoned change. Just the same as he did every day.

Eddy didn't earn a lot mopping floors and emptying waste baskets. Not even with a union card in his wallet. But there were perks, like paid holidays and a dental plan—and the handful of change that he took home every day. Some of it he picked up off the floors when he was cleaning. Most of it he found in the vending machines—the coffee machines, soda machines and candy machines that displayed their goodies in the clutches of big, rotating metal coils. Eddy had learned early on that people who were hanging around in the hospital were often very distracted; they cared about things more important than the nickel they were owed after they bought a package of stale pretzels. So he got

into the habit of checking the change slots on his way home. Sometimes he found enough for a candy bar. Sometimes, on a good day, he found much more.

He was having a *very* good day. There was a considerable amount of jingle in his pockets by the time he reached the ring of pay phones by the exit. Like someone caught in a revolving door, Eddy circled the stand, flipping open each of the scarred chrome change doors as he moved past. On the last one, he got lucky. His finger caught the rough edge of something that turned out to be a quarter.

"Excellent," he said as he slipped the notched quarter into his pocket with the rest of the day's take. Without stopping to count his scavenged loot, he knew that he had enough to buy himself lunch. He could tell by the weight of the coins in his pocket.

Eddy liked a place on Fifth Street called "Boomerangs." It was more of a fast-food counter than a restaurant, the kind of place that had standing-height tables bolted to the floor and no chairs. They made a better-than-good loaded cheeseburger, and when Eddy's number came up on the digital "Now Serving" sign, he ordered one with extra pickles and fried onions. When the swarthy guy who was running the lunchtime show slid his tray across the counter, Eddy could already see grease oozing out of the folds in the foil wrapper. He knew that the white paper lining the inside of the foil would be transparent by the time he unwrapped his burger. Usually, that was enough to make his mouth water. But, for some strange reason, his appetite, along with his good mood, had melted away in the heat during his walk from the hospital. Briefly, Eddy considered asking for a bag to transport his Boomerang burger home. It wouldn't be as good if he ate it later, though, not even if he microwaved it. So he found himself a spot at the counter by the window, set down the orange plastic tray and peeled back the foil.

He took one of his usual wolf-like bites and choked.

At first, he wasn't that scared. He ate like an animal— his girlfriend often said so—so he was no stranger to having the odd bit of food tickle the wrong pipe. But when he tried to cough and found that he couldn't suck any air past the blockage, Eddy knew that he was in frightening, unfamiliar territory. He felt his lungs begin to burn, and his head filled with pressure. *Choking isn't so much about what's in your throat,* he thought, crazily. *It's all the bad business above and below it.*

He knocked his tray to the floor, and the other customers turned their attention toward him. He was heaving mightily by that time, nearly convulsing as his body tried to right itself, and people were backing away in horror. A couple of customers abandoned their half-eaten lunches and quickly left as if they had decided that going hungry was a small price to pay for not having to watch some guy choke to death. For once, Eddy wished that he was back at work, surrounded by the stethoscope-wearing aristocracy who treated him like he was nothing but who knew exactly what to do in such a situation.

Of course, they didn't have the market cornered on such knowledge.

Eddy was on his knees on the floor, his vision getting grainy and dark, when he felt someone slip their arms under his. The person lifted him up and hugged him tightly from behind. Suddenly, he felt a rock-hard fist driving into his gut and a short, sharp blow that would leave him bruised and sore for a week. A huge, partially chewed hunk of gray meat landed on the tile in front of Eddy with a sickening, wet plop. Then, miraculously, he felt air whooshing into his lungs.

"Chew better," said a voice from behind him.

"I plan to from now on," Eddy gasped out in a thin, scratchy voice.

"No. I say 'Are choo better?'" corrected the stranger. Eddy turned around to see that he had been saved by the olive-skinned cook who had served him his burger.

"Yeah," Eddy nodded. "I could use a glass of water, though." His throat felt as if it had been scoured with steel wool. To his astonishment, however, the cook shook his head briskly. He pointed to the wall of vending machines where customers got their own beverages while they were waiting for their food to come out of the fryer.

"Use macheen!" he barked before going back around to the service side of the counter. The cook was done with him; Eddy could feel it. If nobody was going to die, then he had other fish to fry. Literally.

Eddy was thinking uncharitable thoughts as he plugged his remaining change into one of the machines. But when the final coin went in (Eddy felt the tiny nick and thought it interesting that the last quarter he spent was also the last one he had collected) and the bottle of spring water dropped down into the tray, his emotional state shifted dramatically. Suddenly, he was amazed that he could have been feeling anything other than gratitude.

I could have died, he thought. *That guy saved my life. Who cares about the rest?*

Eddy went home feeling a tremendous affection for the dark man in the stained white apron. He was, after all, just another grunt, doing another menial job. Someone not unlike himself.

The afternoon heat had become absolutely oppressive, and Carol asked herself for the 10th time why she had left the air-conditioned comfort of her apartment. It was a good question, but she also had a good answer: the four walls had been closing in on her, forcing her to think ridiculously morbid thoughts. When she lay down on the sofa and mused that it was precisely the size that a coffin would be, she realized that it was time to leave. She could forward her calls to her cell phone. There was really no need to stay in and torture herself while she waited for the news.

Once she was outside, however, she saw things differently. Once she had walked for a dozen sweltering blocks with rivulets of perspiration running down her back, she was sure that she had simply found a different method of torture. She was being baked alive—the word "cremated" crossed her mind—and it made her long for the relatively easier-to-bear mental punishment she had been inflicting upon herself at home.

She began to feel faint at one point and walked into a greasy burger place in search of a drink. Vending machines lined one wall, and Carol plugged some coins into one that dispensed plastic bottles of spring water. The drink that she got was ice-cold and instantly refreshing, but Carol's mood grew darker than ever. The machine had owed her 35 cents in change and had coughed out only a quarter. It wasn't even a good quarter—it had a rough little gouge in it. Something like that had to be a bad omen; she felt sure of it.

Carol left the burger joint holding the nasty quarter and was still clutching it in her sweaty palm when she found a vacant bench near the entrance to the park. The bench was nicely shaded by a leafy tree and felt 10 degrees cooler than the rest of the roasting world. Carol settled down with a sigh and came to a decision. She would wait in that spot until either her phone call came or the sun moved so much that the shade slipped away. Both were certainties. The sun always crawled across the sky, even on days like this when time seemed to be at a standstill. And she had been promised—*promised*—a phone call from her doctor today, a call with the results of those tests.

"Spare change, lady?"

Carol looked up and saw one of the panhandlers whom the police were always vowing to keep out of the parks. The man was rough-looking, dirty and wearing layers of clothing, despite the heat. Carol wondered if he was carrying around everything that he owned on his back. She felt sympathy, but it was heavily laced with loathing, and she flinched when the man stretched out his open hand toward her.

"Please, can you spare a little change?"

Carol's cell phone rang then, and she was suddenly overwhelmed by a sense of doom. She was dying, she was sure of it...

"Hello?" she answered.

"Spare change?"

Carol listened numbly to the faraway receptionist asking her to hold for her doctor, and she looked up at the bum who was still pleading for a handout with his foggy, bloodshot eyes. And she realized at once that the only thing worse than having her terminal condition confirmed would be having it confirmed in front of him.

She was still holding the damned quarter from the machine that had ripped her off. Frantically, she thrust her arm forward and dropped the coin into the man's outstretched hand. He nodded his thanks and began to move away.

The relief that Carol felt was overwhelming. Oddly enough, the feeling washed over her even before her doctor came on the line, saying, "Well, it's not as bad as we thought..."

Alfred had just managed to collect enough change to buy a bottle of cheap wine when one of his headaches came on. It happened fast and it was a bad one. He had suffered enough of them to know two things for sure: he had to find a place to sleep and he couldn't have a drink for a few hours. If he did drink before the pain started to subside, the headache would be worse. Blindingly worse. Knowing this didn't take away the craving, though, and it didn't give him strength in the face of temptation. He had the money. He *knew* he would buy the wine. And then he would be in a state of agony that could last a day or more. Alfred knew that there was only one way to save himself from that experience.

There was a kid, a young guy of about 20, sitting by the big fountain strumming a scarred-up guitar. He was moaning and mumbling some folkie tune about free love and flowers that Alfred, being more of a blues fan, didn't understand or care for. But it didn't matter. He walked up to the kid's open guitar case and in one shaky, generous gesture rid himself of both his money and the devilish temptation. Every coin from every pocket went into the case—including the very last quarter he had bummed, the one from the woman who looked ready to explode from some terrible tension inside her. Alfred put it all in so he wouldn't have to wrestle with himself over whether to buy a bottle that would result in pure misery.

The young guy looked bewildered but thanked Alfred with a nod. Alfred didn't respond. He was walking away, thinking of his next hurdle. He needed a place—best if it was out of the heat—where he could nurse the pulsing black pain that had taken root in his head. The shelters didn't usually let anyone in before dark, but maybe if he explained and they saw that he was sober…

He stopped.

In the time it had taken him to shuffle a dozen steps away from the fountain, the headache had begun to lift. Alfred stood still, frozen in wonder as the pain left in waves. Then, just as suddenly as it had appeared, it was gone. Completely, miraculously gone.

Alfred glanced back once at the folkie's guitar case and sighed. He wished that he had his money back for the wine. But his relief far outweighed his regret.

It was early. The park was filled with people and not one of them, that he could see, was wearing a badge.

"Plenty of change for the asking," he told himself, and he walked on.

It was getting late in the afternoon, the park was starting to empty out and Chris hadn't had a single contribution since the weird old rummy had turned out his pockets.

Small wonder, he thought. He'd been playing lousy since then, hitting plenty of flat notes, and one of his guitar strings was thudding like a piece of twine. Chris wondered if it was the heat that was getting to him, but he wondered more about the kid who had been sitting on the edge of the fountain, staring at him, for more than an hour. Freaky kids like that could put a whammy on a guy; he knew it.

He strummed the opening chords of an old standard that he'd played a thousand times, opened his mouth to sing and found himself unable to remember the first line.

It was the final straw. He stopped playing, lay his guitar flat across his lap and looked directly at the boy.

"Hey, kid," Chris said in a voice full of forced friendliness. "Why don't you get yourself some ice cream?" He scooped a handful of coins out of his battered guitar case and tossed them the boy's way. The kid's chubby, sunburned face lit up.

"Thanks!" he said. "Thanks a lot!" The kid seemed so genuine and looked so grateful to be picking up money off the pavement—money that some jerk had *thrown* at him—that Chris experienced a moment of shame. It felt bad but not so bad that he didn't notice the cloud that lifted when the kid ran off looking for a vendor.

Chris picked up his guitar with renewed confidence and tucked into an old Arlo Guthrie song. The first woman to walk by tossed a buck into his case. Chris smiled at her, kept singing and thought to himself that you could just never tell where luck—good or bad—was coming from.

The kid had been crying a little bit. His face was red in a way that wasn't all sunburn, and his eyes had gotten puffy. He was miserable, holding an empty ice-cream cone in one sticky fist. The scoop of double-chocolate fudge that had perched there minutes before had been lost down a storm drain, all because of a ratty-looking magpie that had swooped past and startled him.

He checked his pockets. Only one quarter left, a nicked one, which wouldn't even come close to buying another ice cream. The kid looked at the coin in his hand and then up at the offending bird. For a moment, he appeared to be considering something. He seemed to weigh the quarter in his hand. Then he raised up his pitching arm.

Though he was not a mean boy by nature, he felt much, *much* better when he saw the coin ricochet off the bird's scruffy head.

Sally put her back out a little when she bent over to pick up the quarter that was lying beside the dead bird. She winced as she straightened up and reminded herself that, at her age, she needed to be more careful. About bending, that was, not about picking up coins that were lying next to disease-infested scavengers. Her pension didn't stretch the whole way from one month to the next, and she was in no position to be turning up her nose at a quarter, whether it came mint condition from a bank teller or dirty from beside a dead magpie.

She was on her way home. The heat had let up a little, enough that her cramped two-room apartment would be bearable for the evening. Not so much that Sally felt like firing up her hot plate, though. No, supper on this night was going to come from the take-out pizza joint that was just around the corner from her walk-up. They sold slices as big as dinner plates there. The cheese and mushroom was Sally's favorite.

By the time she reached the pizza place, though, her back was starting to spasm painfully and she wondered whether she should even bother to stop. She was thinking more of her old, patched recliner than she was of food. But Sally knew that she had to eat something, and there was no sense paying the delivery charge when she was walking right past. So she went in, placed her order and watched as a muscular, gray-haired man whose name tag read *Silvio* cut a generous, glistening wedge out of one of his pies.

"One slice cheese and mushroom—be $4.25."

Sally took four dollars out of her purse and then, from her pocket, produced the quarter that she had picked up on the street. The man put the cash in the register, then held out the box that contained Sally's supper. As she reached across the counter to receive it, she felt something pop in her spine. Relief radiated out to every point in her body.

"Oh!" she said. "Oh, yes!"

When the man eyed Sally suspiciously, she stammered out an embarrassed "thank you" and quickly left. Once she was out on the street, when the door of the pizza joint had closed behind her, she began to chuckle.

She was thinking that fast food had more health benefits than the experts would ever admit.

Silvio tried everything he could think of. He checked his inventory, cleaned out the shelf below the cash register and made a batch of calzone. He kept busy, but he just couldn't shake the feeling of doom. It felt as though the *diavolo* himself was looking over his shoulder.

The sensation stayed with him for nearly two hours until the delivery kid, Ralphie, came in to start his shift. Then, as Silvio was giving Ralphie his cash float—a belt with little metal canisters that he had loaded with coins from the till—something changed. Silvio watched the kid walk out the back door holding his first two orders and felt his sense of foreboding leave as quickly as it had come.

Goose walked over my grave, he thought. It's what his old mother would have said.

It was nearly 10 PM and starting to cool off when Ralphie pulled up in front of the house on River Street with the extra-large, double-pepperoni, double-sausage, extra-cheese order. It was his 11th delivery in two hours. Nobody wanted to cook when it was hot.

He slid out of the driver's seat of his beat-up old car and sprinted up the front walk balancing the big thermal envelope that kept the pizza sizzling. People who were anxiously waiting for their food to arrive liked to see a little hustle. It made them feel that their cravings were important to Ralphie. Usually, it made them part with a bit of their change, offer up a little tip. But nobody had been tipping him that night, no matter how enthusiastically he jogged up to their doors. He was having no good luck at all.

Ralphie rang the bell. When the door opened, he knew instantly that his luck wasn't ready to change yet. The man didn't look like the kind of guy who usually tipped. Sure enough, when Ralphie handed him his change—a fiver, two dimes and a quarter—the guy didn't even tell him to keep the silver. He grabbed it as greedily as he had grabbed his heart-attack special and then pushed the door closed.

"Enjoy your pizza," Ralphie muttered as he turned and started back down the walk toward his idling car. But he was surprised to note that he didn't feel as bitter as he had expected to. Instead, he was starting to feel rather philosophical about his unprofitable evening. True, he'd had a little run of bad luck—but it was nothing, really; it was nothing compared to what some people endured. He noticed then that the car parked in the customer's driveway had a badly crumpled fender and that the lawn was being overtaken by fairy ring. The picture window at the front of the house had been broken and patched up with cardboard, and the big elm tree in the front yard was turning gray with decay and leaning threateningly toward the roof of the house. This guy who didn't tip was having his own run of bad luck, and it was *much* worse than his own. The realization made him feel grateful for his lot, and his heart lifted.

Ralphie tossed the thermal pack onto the passenger seat and climbed behind the wheel. He put the car in gear and started to whistle.

Suddenly, inexplicably, he felt very optimistic that he would earn a big tip on his next delivery.

🦇

Gavin lifted up the flap of the pizza box and took a big bite out of one slice before he even walked back into the living room. He knew that his doctor would have a coronary of her own if she saw him eating something like that, but he didn't care. His luck had changed, and it was something worth celebrating.

He dropped the box down on top of the coffee table and stuffed the five-dollar bill that the pimply kid had given him back into his wallet. There was a ceramic bowl sitting beside his car keys on the hall table where he usually kept his change. Gavin walked over, shoving more pizza into his mouth as he went, and dropped the silver into it. As the coins were sliding out of his hand, something rough caught his fingertip.

Gavin stopped chewing. He felt a sliver of ice embed itself in his gut. He told himself that it would be paranoid to even look, but then he looked anyway.

It was his quarter. It had the same date, it had the same tiny, jagged notch and the notch was in exactly the same position.

When Gavin screamed, repulsive lumps of mangled sausage and cheese fell out of his mouth.

"I gave you away!" he sobbed. "I GAVE YOU AWAY!"

Howling, he slid down the wall beneath the hooks where he always hung his coats. His tan raincoat, already torn at the pocket, ripped at the collar and landed in a heap on the floor with him.

Outside, a gust of wind hit the rotted-out elm, and it began to tremble.

"My old man used to work with a guy who was kind of simple, you know? A few slices short of a loaf. But he told Dad this freaky story about something that happened after his wife died, and Dad said that while this guy wasn't too bright, he wasn't a liar neither..."

...And The Line Went Dead

The telephone rang. Paul Buswell glanced at his cheap digital watch, saw that it was 8 PM on the nose and smiled. It wasn't a happy smile that went all the way up to his eyes—he hadn't felt a single one of those on his face in the six weeks since Theresa had died. It was more of a smug, bitter smile; it was the kind of smile that said *Aha! I've got you now!* He pushed the "talk" button on the cordless phone that had been clenched in his sweaty hand for half an hour, raised it to his ear and spoke.

"Hello?"

Paul squeezed his eyes shut, bracing himself for the frantic monologue that he knew would follow.

"Paul! PAUL! I can't get home, Paul! I tried, but I can't get there! The train was coming, but I missed it, I don't know how, I don't know what happened, but then it got so dark! Paul! PAUL! I'm scared! Come and get m..."

With a shaking hand, Paul pushed the button a second time to disconnect the call. As always, it took a minute before his heart rate slowed and he was able to take a calm, even breath. Once his nerves had steadied, he pushed his small, round body out of the recliner where he spent his evenings and hurried over to the half-moon telephone table that sat against the wall in the open area where the kitchen morphed into the living room. He switched on the gooseneck lamp over the table and squinted to read the screen on the little white box that had been sitting beside his telephone since lunchtime. Within seconds, a trace of his joyless little smile had crept back.

The woman at the phone company had said that the gadget would work and, lo and behold, it had. The little white box—"call display," she called it—had captured the number of the person who had been torturing him with prank calls for nearly six weeks. It had been five weeks and two days, to be exact. Ever since the bleak afternoon when he had seen his wife put in the ground over at Greenlawn Cemetery.

It had been a terrible, terrible day. Rain beat down steadily from a gunmetal sky while Paul cried like a baby, not caring who saw. Hardly anyone attended the service, anyway. The Buswells had always been an odd-duck sort of couple with few friends. That didn't matter to them, the same way that it didn't matter to them that they were childless. They had each other, and that was plenty. That filled their days. But then, one evening, on her way home from work, Theresa fell off the subway platform into the

path of an oncoming train. Suddenly, Paul had nothing
in his life except four furnished rooms, a part-time job
delivering advertising supplements and a constant,
aching sense of loss. And then, after Theresa was buried,
he had the phone calls.

🦇

The first one came a few hours after the funeral. Paul
had been sitting in his worn recliner, still wearing his one
ill-fitting suit and feeling entirely numb. The ringing of
the telephone had lifted him out of his grief for one mer-
ciful moment; in that tiny sliver of time, Paul forgot that
Theresa was dead and imagined that it was she who was
calling. It was always Theresa who called him at home—
to tell him that she was on her way home from the office
building where she worked as a janitor or to let him
know that she was going to be a little bit late but that he
shouldn't worry. She always had change for the pay
phone because, every morning, Paul would take a couple
of quarters out of his jacket pocket and press them into
the palm of his wife's chubby hand.

"You call now, if you need anything," he would tell her.

He always said it as though he was taking care of her,
but they both knew that it worked the other way around.
It was a comfort to get those phone calls from her, letting
him know exactly how things were. It kept him from getting nervous, the way he sometimes did. So Paul kept giving Theresa quarters. They would collect like ballast in the
bottom of her purse, a weighty reminder that anywhere,
at any time, she could afford to give her husband a call.

So there was that moment, that one glorious moment,
when he thought to himself *that's Theresa,* and he felt his

heart lift. But then reality came crushing back down and Paul realized that it had to be someone else. The coroner. The funeral director. The minister. He had talked to so many solemn strangers over the previous days, it made his head feel fuzzy and thick.

Paul picked up the phone. He barely had a chance to say "hello."

"*Paul? PAUL! Where am I? It's so dark, and I missed the train…*"

It was Theresa. Her voice sounded tinny and distant, but it was recognizable just the same.

"Theresa! What's happening? Theresa!" he had shouted into the telephone, but she didn't seem to hear him. She was screaming too loudly and there was too much static on the line. Then, after only a few seconds, the line went dead. Paul had gone completely pale and was shaking violently. He was perspiring so heavily that an hour later, when he finally took off his suit, the lining was still damp and sour smelling.

On that first night, after the first call, Paul had been so frightened and confused that he was unable to sleep. By the third night, he had noticed that the telephone always rang at exactly 8 PM, the time when Theresa had taken her fatal misstep on the subway platform. And, within a week, he understood that the calls had to be a cruel prank. Paul was gullible and the fellows he worked with were fond of telling him that he wasn't the sharpest knife in the drawer, but he knew when he was being victimized. What he didn't know was what to do about it.

He started out by calling the police. They told him to call the phone company. The phone company told him that they couldn't trace a call unless the police were involved. Paul kept calling back and asking, though, because the calls were so distressing. Eventually, one sympathetic woman at the phone company told him that there was something he could do all on his own. That was when she explained the call display service to Paul. It cost an extra few dollars on his monthly bill, and he had to rent the little white box and figure out how to attach it to his telephone, but it would give him the number of every person who called him, day or night.

"Even the mean ones?" he asked her.

"Even the mean ones," she assured him, and Paul noticed that her voice sounded husky, like she needed to clear her throat.

And so, he got the call display, and he set it up.

And, finally, he had the phone number of the person who was playing the worst trick that anyone had ever played on him.

Paul dialed the number, not knowing what he would say when the party at the other end answered. He knew, somehow, that simply making the call mattered more than how he handled it. He suspected that the horrid woman who could make her voice sound so like Theresa's would stop harassing him as soon as she knew she was exposed. But he was caught utterly off-guard when a man picked up the phone, mumbling something that ended with the phrase "…may I help you?"

"I want to speak to that woman," Paul said after a second or two.

"There's no woman here right now. Who is it that you're looking for?"

There was another stretch of silence as Paul contemplated that.

"Well," he finally said, "then I want to talk to whoever called me five minutes ago. I know it was this number. I suppose it could be a man. Some men can talk really high, like a lady." Paul didn't think that the fellow he was talking to could, though. His voice was too low; it was too gravelly.

"Mister," said the man on the other end, "I can tell you that no one's called you from this number tonight. I work alone here—nobody else comes, goes or uses the phone."

"How can you be sure?" Paul asked. He sounded like a disappointed child.

"I'm sure," said the man. "Believe me, this is the quietest place on earth, especially at night."

"Where's that?" said Paul. "I mean—where are you? I didn't hear exactly what you said when you answered the phone."

"Sorry," the man chuckled. "I tend to mumble a bit. I'm the night watchman here at the cemetery. Greenlawn Cemetery."

And that was when Paul hung up the phone.

The night watchman—Kenny was his name—felt kind of sorry for the fellow who had called. He sounded sad and confused. Maybe even a little on the simple side. But when the line went dead in his ear he simply hung up the phone and went back to flipping the pages of his magazine. There was nothing he could do and, anyway, didn't he have his own mysteries to solve?

Kenny reached across the desk and picked up a quarter that was sitting by the phone. He brushed the dirt off it as he looked up at the ceiling for some clue.

"Gotta be coming from somewhere," he mumbled as he put the coin in a mason jar with all the others. There were more than three dozen of them clinking around in there, all quarters.

He had found one, just after eight o'clock, every night for more than five weeks. They were always covered with bits of fresh, loose earth.

And, always, they were sitting right beside the phone.

*"You know those ghost stories they tell
you at summer camp? Well, I know one
that's real. My uncle used to go to this
place; he had a funny name for it…"*

Camp Wannapoopoo

When Marty was a grown man, 37 years old, he was telling someone about the summer camp of his childhood and was shocked to discover that he couldn't remember its real name.

"It was Wana-something," he said as he scrunched his eyes shut and tried to access the deeper storage of his memory. "A native word." In the politically insensitive year when he had been 10, they called it an Indian word. Not that he and his friends ever referred to the camp by its proper name. Not after the thing that happened to Lanny Bower, anyway. After that, the place had always been referred to, with great snorts of laughter, as "Camp Wannapoopoo."

Lanny Bower was a moon-faced, carrot-topped kid and the worst bully that Marty every knew. He was 12, maybe even pushing 13, during that year when Marty and his friends were 10. He was mean and stupid and bigger than all of the other kids in the fifth grade. He had been held back twice (Marty often imagined the classes who moved on ahead of him breathing a sigh of relief when they learned that Lanny would be staying behind to torture a new group of kids), but after landing in Marty's class, Lanny moved ahead with the group at the end of every year.

"They have to do it. He's outgrowing the desks," was Dave's explanation.

Dave was Marty's best friend. He was a quiet, serious kid with a knack for insights about such things as the lack of available leg room beneath Lanny Bower's desk. He was a tough kid, too—but not in the bullying way that made Lanny tough. Dave was tough because he was brave enough to stand up for himself, even when it meant taking a beating. He had had his front teeth chipped, his glasses broken and, on one memorable occasion, carried his tensor-bandaged arm in a sling for two weeks. Every time, it was because he had refused to knuckle under Lanny or one of his grade-school neanderthal accomplices. And, every time, Dave insisted that it had been worth it.

"Really?" Marty asked him, the time Dave's wrist had been fractured.

"I swear," Dave had said solemnly. There was no need to discuss it further. "I swear" was not something either of the boys said when they were fooling around. "I swear" was dead-serious, stack-of-bibles, on-your-grandmother's-grave stuff.

Marty supposed that it *was* worth it. Dave didn't get respect, exactly, from Lanny and his crew—but sometimes they cut a wide swath around him because he was a nuisance to deal with. It was more efficient for them to bully kids who would give up their lunch money or their candy or their dignity without a fight. Kids who were scared of them. Kids like Marty.

Marty often wished that he had even a small amount of Dave's courage. But, instead, he had his fear of Lanny and the inevitable self-loathing that it generated. Marty's way was to try to be invisible, to make himself small so that he wasn't noticed. And when he did get pushed around a bit, he did his best to laugh it off and pretend that he was a participant and not a victim. It didn't preserve his dignity exactly, but he hoped that it sometimes preserved the *illusion* of it.

The fifth grade had been a particularly long, belittling year for him. It was the year when Lanny learned the difference between a regular wedgie and an atomic wedgie, and Marty had been the recipient of several.

"*Zoom!*" Lanny liked to announce as he delivered that particular form of torture. "*Zoom, zoom, zoom!*"

Tears of pain and rage would be spilling down Marty's face before Lanny even let go of his Jockeys, which made it difficult to salvage any degree of pride. But Dave saw Marty's humiliation and came to his rescue in a typically gutsy, Dave kind of way.

"Lanny," he commented casually during one recess when the majority of the class was within earshot, "you seem to be abnormally interested in other guys' underwear."

That was the incident that resulted in Dave's chipped front tooth. Marty would have gladly given him one of his own teeth as a replacement, but guys didn't say things like that to one another. Instead, Marty told him that the chip made him look tough and said that everyone thought that he was hilarious and asked him if it had been worth it.

"I swear," said Dave, which was all he had to say.

They were looking *so* forward to summer camp that year. It was to be the third year that Marty and Dave would pack their duffel bags and kiss their mothers good-bye and spend two glorious weeks swimming and playing and roasting marshmallows in the wilderness. They were experts at it; they were going to be campers with seniority. After 10 months of living uneasily in Lanny Bower's shadow, the boys were eager to be anywhere where they felt secure. The golden thought of summer kept them going that year, and they discussed it often.

Lanny overheard them once.

"What camp you talkin' about, turd-breath?" he asked. He had come up silently behind Marty and Dave where they sat on the bleachers. He planted the dirty toe of his sneaker in the small of Marty's back to encourage a response.

Marty told him the name of the camp and Lanny brayed laughter.

"Sounds sissy," he said. That was all he said, though, which seemed odd, because Lanny was the kind of guy who would take a piece of personal information like that and abuse it infinitely. But he didn't mention it again, not until Marty and Dave saw him, duffel bag on his shoulder, walking into the parking lot on the perfect, exciting morning when they were about to board the bus that would take them away.

"Thought I'd check out your stupid camp," he said as he butted roughly ahead of them in line. It was the first time Marty had ever been able to pinpoint the exact moment when something special was ruined for him.

Camp, for Lanny, was just a wilderness variation of the schoolyard, and he adapted quickly. Where there was no lunch money to extort, he found things to steal in the care packages that kids had brought from home. Though there were no monkey bars and, therefore, no opportunities to pull down somebody's pants while they dangled from the highest rung, there were plenty of opportunities to shanghai their swimming trunks while they flailed helplessly beneath the cool, green surface of the lake. And Lanny understood instinctively that the punches and noogies and rope burns that were such an effective form of intimidation in the school cloakroom would work every bit as well in a cabin.

The cabins. There were six of them, arranged in a semicircle around the patchy grass field full of fire pits called "the common area." They were low, solid-looking log structures, each large enough for four sets of bunk beds. There were signs hanging over the front doors, each proudly proclaiming the name of the cabin and, by extension, its inhabitants. The names were all purloined from nature; there were Mighty Pines and Soaring Eagles and Wild Wolves. That summer, Marty and Dave were Wandering Bears. By the luck of the draw, or lack thereof, Lanny turned out to be a Wandering Bear as well. The boys weren't surprised. By the time they found out, they were several painful hours into the first day and had already resigned themselves to two weeks of misery.

Beyond the common area was the lake, with a strip of gravelly beach and a roped-off swimming area. There was a float that bobbed in the water some distance

beyond the ropes. It was there for the bigger kids, the
strong swimmers. Marty was a good swimmer, but the
float—that little wooden island that was so far from
shore—frightened him. He always imagined that he
would make it out there and then develop a monster
cramp that would leave him stranded. In this vision, the
other campers would gather on the beach to mock him as
one of the disgusted counselors swam out with a life pre-
server to bring him back in.

At the south end of the shore that capped the common area was the Main Building, which held the cafeteria

and the counselors' offices and had a dock growing out of the west side of its wraparound veranda. The "Main," as everyone called it, had two washrooms with pristine white fixtures. The campers weren't permitted to use them, though—not unless they were suffering from some form of intestinal distress severe enough to keep them in the infirmary. The campers—who were "roughing it," as the counselors liked to remind them—shared three outdoor privies located at the end of three steep, rocky paths in the shadowy, dense woods that crept up to the rear of the cabins.

"Why are there two holes?" Marty had asked Dave the first summer they went away to camp. He was mystified by the side-by-side openings of differing size.

"For different-sized bums," Dave declared. He was an invaluable source of such off-beat information. "They always have a small one, for kids," he added, "so they don't fall in."

That was all it took to make Marty fear the outhouse. He had never before considered that falling in was a possibility, that a person could get lost and die in the foulest place imaginable. From that day forward, he never went to relieve himself without first announcing it, so that someone would know where to start looking if he failed to return. And, once in the outhouse, he would check the size of the holes three or four times before taking the great risk of seating himself. While seated, he always maintained a vigilant watch over the larger hole, as though he believed that something might actually reach up and pull him down into its reeking depths if he relaxed his guard. It was an irrational fear, and Marty knew it. So he never told anyone but Dave. Dave could be counted on to not ridicule or exploit Marty's fears, rational or otherwise. Marty always understood that was why Dave never told him the ghost story before the night he told it to Lanny.

It was their eighth day at camp, and there had been mail. Marty's parents had sent him an economy-sized bag of the dry-roasted peanuts that he loved and a letter saying that they missed him and hoped that he was having fun. He *had* been having fun that day, up until that point. But when Lanny saw that he had a package from home, things changed.

"Whatcha got, butt-wipe?"

Marty was sitting on one of the long benches in the nearly deserted cafeteria. The mail had been handed out after a lunch of franks and beans, and he had lingered there longer than the others, savoring his newsy letter for the second time. He had been too distracted to notice Lanny, two tables over, lagging behind the others, eyeing him as a cat would a mouse.

"Nuthin' much," Marty shrugged and did his best to sound casual. "Letter from home." As he spoke, he stealthily picked up the brown paper parcel that was on the bench beside him and put it in the space between his thighs and the underside of the table. He balanced it there carefully, hoping that from his vantage point, Lanny hadn't been able to see it.

Lanny swaggered over to the opposite side of Marty's table. He swung one lanky, sunburned leg over the bench and plunked himself down.

"Nuthin', huh? That sucks." He rested one elbow on the table, shook his head sympathetically and made a great show of examining a hangnail on one dirty thumb.

Marty didn't know what was coming, but he could feel it coming, and the wait was excruciating. There was nothing to do but wait, however; he had a lap full of contraband peanuts and no place to go. So he pretended that he was cool, that he was just hanging out, enjoying the down time. But as the long, silent seconds ticked by, Marty began to wish fervently for a "do-over." On the playground, when they were shooting marbles or baskets, it was understood that a guy who had been unfairly distracted or had suffered a moment of uncharacteristically bad judgment could occasionally take a second shot. Marty knew that if he had a second shot—his do-over— he would give the package to Lanny straight away and avoid the agonizing tension. It would all be the same in the end anyway.

"You gonna sit here all day, Dumbo?" Lanny was growing tired of the game.

"I don't know. For a while, I guess," Marty said. He could feel the place where his thighs were pressed together beneath the package getting slippery with perspiration.

"Yeah?" Lanny was speaking in a bored tone, but his eyes were narrow and he was scanning the room for adults. "Well, I'm gonna go," he said, "and I'm gonna take *this* with me." He reached under the table and snatched the parcel away. Then he stood up, leaned forward and delivered a painful jab to Marty's left shoulder.

"Teach ya to lie," he said. He looked in the package then and started to laugh. "Over stupid peanuts!" he added as he sauntered out of the room.

It wasn't until Lanny had left that Marty saw Dave standing in the doorway that led to the kitchen. Marty quickly wiped his hands across his eyes and tried to look cool.

"Thought you were playing ball," he said in his oh-so-casual voice.

"It was my turn to help clean up," Dave replied.

Marty didn't know how long his friend had been standing there, but he guessed that it was long enough. Dave had that look, that same calm, intense look that Marty had seen on his face a few times before. Usually, it preceded some incident that resulted in a chipped tooth or broken glasses or a bandaged arm. Something was brewing beneath Dave's quiet exterior, and knowing that made Marty wish more than ever that he had given up the peanuts immediately.

Lights out at 10 PM was the rule at summer camp. It was a rule largely ignored and seldom enforced. Sing-alongs and stories around the flickering campfire were only half of the evening's fun as far as the campers were concerned. The other half took place after they were tucked into their bunks for the night. That was when the flashlights and comic books would come out, along with the candy and the kind of stories that fresh-faced camp counselors deemed inappropriately frightening. Marty was usually an enthusiastic participant in the bedtime sessions, but on the night after Lanny stole his care package, he wasn't in the mood. He simply lay in his bunk with his hands folded behind his head, listening to the raucous conversation of the other Wandering Bears and to the insistent crunching noise that came from the bunk above him as Lanny finished the last of the roasted peanuts.

It was nearly midnight, and the boys were beginning to grow quiet when Lanny balled up the plastic bag with his meaty hands and tossed it down onto Marty's bunk.

"Here, loser," he said. "You can have what's left."

What was left was nothing more than crumbs and a powdery salt residue. Marty batted the empty bag aside and said nothing. There had been more than two pounds of peanuts. He would have made it last the week. Lanny had vacuumed them up over the course of a few hours.

Not surprisingly, they were working their way south.

"Gotta go for a dump," Lanny announced as he climbed down from the upper bunk. He was almost out the door of the cabin when Dave spoke.

"Watch out for the ghost," he said nonchalantly. He flipped the page of his *Spiderman* comic then, but when Marty looked across the room, he could tell that Dave was only pretending to read.

Lanny paused with his hand on the door latch.

"Right!" he snorted. But after a beat of silence, he said "What ghost?" in a tone that was just a little less confident.

Dave kept his eyes on his comic for a second or two. Then he looked innocently up at Lanny.

"Huh?" he said, as though he had already forgotten the subject at hand. But his memory returned to him in convenient good time. "Oh, right—the ghost," he nodded. "Never mind. You probably don't believe that stuff."

"I don't!" Lanny sneered. "Those fairy stories are for you morons. I just want to know what you were yakking about, is all."

Dave turned another page. He took a deep breath. Then, finally, he turned his full attention to Lanny. He stared at him for a moment or two, as if sizing up his ability to handle something.

"Well," he said, "it's just some story. I overheard some of the counselors talking about it. But I think probably it's true, 'cause they were acting weird, you know? Scared, I mean."

"What'd they say?" Lanny asked. It came out as more of an order than a question.

Dave swung his legs off the edge of his bunk. He rested his elbows on his knees and folded his hands together. Marty recognized that he was about to stop teasing Lanny; he was ready to share the story. He rolled over onto his side so he was facing Dave, so he wouldn't miss anything. He saw the other boys subtly moving to focus their attention as well.

"Here's the thing," Dave began. "They said that the outhouses are haunted."

Dave paused for dramatic effect. Marty heard the soft whisper of someone quickly sucking in his breath and felt his own stomach flutter with a mixture of fear and excitement.

"I guess a few years back there was this camp counselor who went crazy. He really bugged out, you know? But nobody knew it because he was going around acting all cool, even though inside he was just—*twisted apart.* Then, one night, one of the campers disappears. A kid about our age. At lights out, he was there, and in the morning, he was gone. His friend said that he had gone out to the toilet, sometime in the middle of the night. But the friend fell asleep again before he got back.

"Of course, it turned out that he never *did* get back. The psycho counselor got him on the path out back and murdered him in cold blood."

"How did they know?" whispered a chubby blond boy named Miles who occupied the bunk above Dave's.

"'Cause they found the kid—eventually," Dave explained. "They found him in pieces. The counselor cut him up into a dozen body parts and dumped a few of them into each of the privies. Then he threw a bunch of lime down the holes and went back to his quarters. The next morning, at breakfast, he slit his own throat with a butcher knife in front of the whole camp."

"What were they having?" breathed Miles, whose every day at camp was defined by the cafeteria menu.

"Pancakes." Dave spoke solemnly and without hesitation. "Word has it that most of 'em went to waste."

Lanny still had his hand on the door handle. He was standing stiffly, uncomfortably, and kept shifting his weight from one foot to the other. But he made no move to leave the cabin.

"You said there was a ghost," he griped.

Dave nodded gravely.

"Oh, there is," he said. "It's the murdered kid. They fished what was left of him out of the holes, but his spirit doesn't know that. And he's lonely. The counselors said that on nights just like this—when there's no moon—he haunts the woods around the outhouses. They said that if he sees you going, he follows. And then, when you sit down, he grabs you! He pulls you down into the rotting muck, to keep him company for all eternity."

The cabin was entirely silent as the boys absorbed the chilling finale of Dave's story. Marty's heart beat so

loudly that he worried the others would be able to hear its frightened rhythm. It was as though Dave's story had been custom-made to terrify him, playing as it did on his most private fear. But when he looked up, he could see that he wasn't the only one who had been scared.

Lanny was still standing by the door, and he still had his hand on the latch. But he appeared to be holding the door tightly closed rather than preparing to open it. And he was pale; even in the shadowy, yellow cast of the boys' flashlights, Marty could see that the color had drained out of his face.

Dave was lying down again, flipping calmly through the last pages of his comic.

"Thought you had to make a trip out back," he said. Though there was nothing in the tone of his voice to indicate it, it sounded like a dare.

Marty looked at Lanny. He could see the muscles of his jaw clenching and releasing, clenching and releasing. The muscles of his backside clenched and remained clenched. He was awkwardly posed, with his rear end tucked in and his pelvis thrust slightly forward.

"Nah," Lanny said, when he finally responded to Dave. "Your windbag story took so long, it crawled back up. I shoulda just gone before you started blabbing." He climbed back into his bunk, moving as slowly and stiffly as an old man.

The flashlights winked out one by one, and the campers all snuggled deeply under their blankets. It was the time when Lanny usually liked to flop around like a dying fish, torturing Marty with the fear that the upper bunk would eventually break under his thrashing bulk, and Lanny would kill him by falling on top of him. But on that night, there was no movement in Lanny's bunk. Marty barely noticed. He was too busy obsessing about his raw, renewed fear of the outhouses. The images were so fresh, so vivid, he began to imagine that he could smell the reeking depths of composting...

"Aw, man, who cut one?"

A chorus of protesting groans rose up in the cabin, and Marty realized that the foul smell was not a product of his imagination.

"Not me," he said.

"Me neither," came six other voices in staggered unison. Then all was silent for a time as the boys waited for the air to clear.

It didn't.

"Come on," moaned one of the campers. "Take the silent bombs outside, wouldja?"

Dave switched on his flashlight and bounced the light off the low ceiling of the cabin. It was a jaundiced, low-wattage interrogation light.

"Who's guilty?" he asked. "Confess now and we'll go easy on ya."

There was no reply. Most conspicuously, there came no reply or comment of any sort from Lanny Bower's bunk. It was utterly unnatural. Lanny would normally have been the first to log in with a threat or degrading comment. But he said nothing, which spoke volumes.

Dave focused his flashlight on Lanny's bunk.

"Lanny," Dave said very slowly, as though he was in great shock. "Lanny, did you have a bit of an *accident?*"

At that moment, everyone understood that was exactly what had happened. The smell was too heavy, too pungent, too insistent to be the result of someone passing a bit of gas. It just hung in the air, like a permanent noxious cloud. Lanny Bower had deposited a big, old, peanut-packed fudge bar in his briefs and everybody knew it.

There was a muffled snort of laughter from the rear of the cabin. It was all that was needed to set Lanny off.

"It's *your* fault!" he roared at Dave. "You and your stupid *story!* You're gonna pay!"

Marty felt the frame of the bunk bed lurch as Lanny leapt off. He gagged on the smell, which, released from the containment of Lanny's bedcovers, had exploded in intensity. And he turned to warn Dave.

"Run!" he yelled, although he saw immediately that the warning had been unnecessary. Dave was out the door by the time the word was out of Marty's mouth. He was gutsy, but not foolish. He would get out of taking his licks if he could.

Lanny bolted out of the cabin after Dave. There was one frozen moment, after the blond kid named Miles switched on his own flashlight and before Lanny disappeared into the dark outdoors, when Marty glimpsed the bully's face. What he saw there was like nothing he had ever seen there before. It was *fury.*

Lanny had always been what Marty thought of as a happy bully. He intimidated others because he took genuine pleasure in it; it was his special talent, not unlike the talent that other kids had for basketball or math problems. It wasn't unusual to see him wearing a big, dopey grin when he was stealing something or punching someone or vandalizing their property. It was what he did best; he *enjoyed* it. But that night, when Lanny barreled out the door in pursuit of Dave, there was no grin. There was nothing on his face but a volatile mixture of humiliation and rage, a murderous combination in someone who held a 30-pound advantage over his intended victim.

Suddenly, Marty thought that Dave might lose more than part of a tooth. He thought that he might break something that healed a lot more slowly than a wrist, and he thought that this time, it wouldn't be worth it. He kicked off the tangle of blankets that pinned down his legs, grabbed his flashlight and hit the rough floorboards of the cabin running. He was terrified, but he couldn't let Dave take that kind of beating. Especially when he knew, deep down, that Dave would be taking it for him. He lurched out of the cabin and let the door swing shut behind him.

The darkness outside was absolute. Dave had been right—it was a moonless night, with a veil of high cloud that kept even the stars from peeking through. Marty switched on his flashlight. It barely penetrated the gloom, but he swung it in a wide arc in the direction of the common area anyway, hoping to see the weak beam reflect off someone. He saw nothing, but after a moment, he heard something. It was a crackling of underbrush. It was coming from behind the cabins.

The muscles in Marty's legs felt suddenly slack and useless. He didn't want to follow Dave and Lanny there. Not after that story. But then he remembered the look on Lanny's face, the violent, animal look, and he thought of Dave, who had more guts than anyone should carry around in a skinny little 10-year-old body. Marty took a deep breath, rounded the corner of the cabin and followed the twisting, rocky path into the woods.

The silence there was as dense as the darkness. Marty crept along in his bare feet, unblinking, barely breathing lest the sigh of his own respiration mask some other sound. The dim circular glow cast by his flashlight flickered twice and he knew that the batteries were at their end. He suddenly wondered how he could have wasted them reading comic books in the safety of the cabin. Now they were going to burn out when he really needed them, when he was in the ink black forest that hid both a maniac and a ghost.

"Dave?" Marty called out his friend's name. Almost instantly, he realized that Dave couldn't answer him without giving away his position to Lanny. "Lanny?" he said then, taking a different approach. Nothing but silence. Marty began to fear two things simultaneously and equally. He feared that he had incorrectly guessed the direction that the other boys had taken and that Lanny was at that moment beating the life out of Dave behind the Main Building or down on the beach. And he feared that he was utterly alone, in the woods, on a night when the ghostly camper was sure to be there as well.

At that moment, the flickering beam of Marty's flashlight bounced back at him in twin oval reflections. Marty jumped but quickly recognized that he was looking at the lenses of Dave's glasses. Dave, who was crouching in the thick bushes beside the trail, as still as a stopped clock, looked up at Marty with desperate eyes. He held one finger across his lips, begging mutely for silence and secrecy.

But when Marty's nostrils picked up the sharp scent of excrement, he knew that it was too late.

There was a roar from behind Marty then, and Lanny blasted past him on the trail. *He was following me!* Marty realized with horror as he was roughly shoved out of the way. Dave sprang up and tried to run, but he was too tangled in branches to make a quick getaway. Lanny grabbed him by one arm, threw him down and, instantly, was on top of him.

"I'll show ya!" he bellowed. "I'll show ya to tell stupid stories!"

"Get off!" Marty was pulling at the back of Lanny's t-shirt, trying to peel him away from Dave. It didn't work. Lanny brought up his fist—that big, meaty fist, the one with the hangnail on the thumb, Marty remembered—and brought it down on the fleshy part of Dave's arm. He brought it up again and aimed it at his ribs. Brought it up again and hammered it into his stomach. Dave made soft little "oof" sounds as his breath was punched out of him again and again. Lanny was making sounds of his own; strangled, choking, mucousy noises. Marty eventually realized that as he was beating Dave, he was crying.

That was more frightening than anything. For a guy like Lanny, tears were the greatest loss of control imaginable greater even than what had happened in the cabin. Marty knew right then that Lanny was going to keep pounding Dave until he was bleeding both inside and out; he was going to pound him until he was unconscious or even dead.

Marty lifted up his flashlight.

"Leave him alone!" he screamed, and he brought it down like a club on top of Lanny's skull.

There was a crunch of splintering plastic. The light blinked off. Lanny howled out in pain and fury, but he didn't go down. Instead, he turned to focus his rage on Marty, and what Marty saw in his contorted features was pure, raw hatred. He felt panic rising up inside of him, but behind it, there was another feeling; there was a sense that something was not right. The flashlight was gone, lying in the brush somewhere with two dead batteries and a broken lens. That had been the only light and, yet, Marty could *see* Lanny's face. He could see it clearly, illuminated in a cool, blue, wavering glow that reminded him of the aquarium in his bedroom at home. As Marty realized that, Lanny's pale, underwater expression began to change. He was looking over Marty's shoulder then, and whatever he saw there was melting his wrath, replacing it with something that Marty couldn't pinpoint right away because it was an expression that did not look at home on a bully's face.

Terror, he finally understood. It was terror.

Marty felt Lanny's thick fingers first loosen their grip on his arm and then slip away entirely. He saw him shrink back, his mouth forming a round "O" of horror and his larynx bobbing spastically in his throat. He tripped over Dave's sprawling legs and fell down hard on his backside, setting off a fresh burst of stench from the foul bomb he was carrying around in his pants. His gaze remained fixed on the point behind Marty's shoulder.

There was a rustling, a bit of movement, and Marty saw Dave struggling to sit up. He saw Dave's eyes, wide and staring, focused in the same direction. He saw his face illuminated by the same swimmy blue light. Marty didn't want to turn around; he would have given up dry-roasted peanuts for the rest of his life to not have to turn around, but he did. And then he felt the muscles of his own face fall slack with fear.

For there, not more than 30 feet up the path, stood the ghostly camper.

He was just a kid—certainly no older than Marty and Dave were and maybe even a little younger. His features were clearly defined although he seemed to be no more than a concentrated form of that bluish aquarium light. Marty could see so many normal "kid" things about him, from the bad porridge-bowl haircut to the way his shirt was only half tucked in. But there were more things that weren't normal at all, things that shouldn't ever be associated with childhood. It was the combination—the juxtaposition of things wholesome and vile—that seemed so profane.

The kid's eyes weren't eyes at all; they were gloomy sockets housing pinpoints of red light that seemed to originate from somewhere deep within his skull. His clothing—shorts and an official camp t-shirt almost identical to the ones the boys wore—was smeared with dark streaks of filth. And then there were his sneakers, his mucky, once-white sneakers which did not quite seem to touch the ground.

The ghost extended one skinny, translucent hand toward them. His tiny red firelight pupils were trained on Lanny. His lips moved and then the voice, out of sync with its body, arrived.

"*Come,*" it said.

It was the voice not of a child, but of a *child-thing*, strangulated, sodden and choked with rotting matter. As the single word drifted past him, Marty gagged on an odor 10 times as loathsome as the product of Lanny's bowels.

"*Come.*" Again, the wave of putrid air. But this time, the apparition beckoned more insistently and began to creep toward the boys, skimming evenly over the rough surface of the path. As it moved, there was a rustling of branches and leaves. Marty saw the bushes shrinking away as though they were conscious beings, repelled by the glowing form.

Lanny was terrified out of his shocked state.

"Oh, no!" he shrieked. "No way! No way!" He scrambled backward like a crab until he was able to push himself to his feet. Then he ran. Marty could hear Lanny's big feet pounding the dirt, retreating into the distance, but he didn't turn around to watch him go.

He was watching the advancing ghostly camper. He wanted to run too, and he thought that he could, even though his legs were filled with lead. But Dave was still on the ground and by the time he was able to get up by himself...

Well, Marty figured that by that time, the camper would have himself a new friend. Someone to keep him company, way down in the desecrated place where no one else wanted to visit. And, terrified as he was, Marty couldn't let that happen.

"Let's go!" he hissed at Dave as he grabbed his arm. "Come on!" He pulled his friend to his feet and tried to get him moving. But Dave was holding back; he was digging his heels into the soft earth at the side of the path and saying something that Marty couldn't understand.

"It's okay!" he was saying. "Marty, look! It's okay!"

Marty did look then. He put his panic on hold just long enough to glance up the path. Then he spun around frantically, searching the entire area. He saw nothing. There was no watery-light entity, there was no Lanny, there was no one with him but Dave, who was hunched over and gingerly holding the place on his side that had taken the worst of the rock-hard punches.

"I think we can go back to the cabin now," Dave said.

So they did.

Lanny was waiting for them, sitting on the single, worn, wooden step that led to the cabin's door. He had changed his pants in the time that it had taken Marty to help Dave limp back down the path. His face had changed, too. It was still tear-streaked and full of shame, but the menace was gone.

"You don't tell nobody about this," he told them. "Not ever."

"As long as you leave us alone," said Marty.

There was a flash of anger in Lanny's eyes and the muscles of his jaw seemed to tighten. But he nodded—it was a curt, almost imperceptible movement, but enough to establish that a deal had been struck.

Lanny stood up and went back into the cabin then. The door had barely shut behind him when Dave began clapping Marty enthusiastically on the back.

"That was so cool!" he said. "You saved my butt and you kicked his! You're like a super hero!"

"Really?" asked Marty, who wasn't accustomed to such overwhelming admiration.

"I swear!" said Dave.

It was all he had to say. For that one moment, Marty felt powerful and not afraid of anything. He thought that the next day, he might just swim out to the float.

The sixth grade turned out to be an excellent year for all the Wandering Bears. Lanny Bower did leave them alone; he had no choice, given the dangerous knowledge of the chock-full-o-peanuts special that each of them possessed. The secret was kept within the group, but every once in a while, when there was no one but Wandering Bears present, some wit would inevitably blurt out "Camp Wannapoopoo!" and send them all into convulsions. They never called their summer retreat by its proper name again, and they kept their lunch money—every nickel of it—from that point forward.

Marty and Dave kept their part of the secret, too. They never told anyone about the ghost or about the way Lanny had run like a blubbering coward in its presence. Occasionally, when it was just the two of them sitting around, the subject would come up. One night, when they were watching a scary movie on TV, Dave confessed to making up much of the story he had told Lanny. Another time, during a dull museum field trip, Marty admitted that he had come close to soiling his own underwear at the moment when he first saw the ghost.

But they didn't talk about it much. And, the truth was Marty didn't want to talk about it at all. He didn't even want to think about it. There were enough times already when he awoke from a deep sleep with his heart caught in his throat, certain that he could see two pinpoints of hellfire glaring at him from the cool blue depths of his aquarium.

Eventually, Marty learned to coexist with his fear. More accurately, he grew up and displaced it with workaday worries about things like his debt load and cholesterol count. And, as the years passed and his life filled up with increasingly distracting details, the events of that night took on the fuzzy, unreliable quality of a childhood memory. It got to the point where Marty wondered what percentage of it was real and what percentage was fiction; he was sure that he must have enhanced the experience with vivid comic-book details from his fertile 10-year-old imagination. He grew quite comfortable with that explanation. It didn't challenge his adult belief system and it didn't keep him awake at night. It worked—until the day he ran into Lanny Bower.

Marty had been coming out of a café on Main Street. He and his son—a boy nearly as old as Marty had been that long-ago summer—were in town for a few days to visit Marty's folks. They had just stepped out on the sidewalk; they were squinting in the sunlight and unwrapping the cellophane from the green-and-white striped mints that the waitress had put on top of their tab when Marty saw him. It was Lanny—25 years older, with less hair and more of a gut, but unmistakably Lanny all the same. Marty recognized the dull, mean eyes and the permanent sneer. He saw the pasty complexion and the carrot tint in the hair that was still clinging to his thick skull. He seemed smaller, though—Marty was surprised to see that he had come to have a good four inches on the bully in the height department. As he was thinking about that, Lanny looked up and saw him.

That time, Marty was quicker to identify the expression on Lanny's face because he had seen it there once before.

Lanny froze in his tracks. He sucked his breath in sharply, then turned abruptly to his right and scurried across the street. He didn't bother to check for traffic and one driver blared his horn in protest. Lanny jabbed his middle finger into the air as his own form of protest, but he kept his head down and his pace up. He didn't turn or look back even once and, eventually, he disappeared inside an arcade on the other side of the street.

"Who's that weird guy?" asked Marty's son as he popped his mint into his mouth.

Marty shook his head.

"Just a guy I used to know," he said.

"He looks scared," said the boy. *He lookth thcared* was how the words came out, around the mint.

"He does, doesn't he?" Marty agreed. Lanny had looked scared. Not embarrassed, as a guy might be if he was remembering a mess he made in his pants a quarter of a century earlier, but scared. Scared, as though running into Marty had reminded him of some terrifying thing that he'd been trying desperately to forget.

And Marty knew then. He knew that his disturbing memory was real, not imaginary, and he understood that, on that night, he had made a bad deal. He had traded in his childish fear of Lanny Bower for a horror that might prove impossible to outgrow. He stood there for a moment, twisting the crinkly candy wrapper in his hand, trying to decide how he would handle this new information.

"Are you coming? You said we could go swimming before supper!"

Marty was pulled back to the present.

"Yes!" he said, trying to sound bright. "Swimming. Race you to the van!"

Marty shared a warm summer afternoon with his son, splashing around in a small lake where he had often played as a child. The boy wasn't a strong swimmer, though, and Marty had to repeatedly coax him to jump from the dock into the water. He held out his arms each time and gestured encouragingly.

"There's nothing to be afraid of," he said at one point. Immediately, he felt like a fraud. There was plenty in the world to be afraid of. Seeing Lanny had reminded him of that. He was reminded of Dave, too, and Marty wondered if his old friend was still as gutsy in the adult world, where one had to face down things like unexpected tax audits and cancerous growths.

Nothing to be afraid of. It was a lie.

All afternoon, he had been scanning the tree line near the shore. He was searching for those soulless twin specs of fiery, red light, and he was very, *very* afraid.

"My grandparents used to run this little country store way back when. Gran thought maybe it was haunted, but Grandpa never wanted to talk about it..."

Molly Goodacre

"Elizabeth, I know you found out about me and Tom. I know, because you don't talk to me these days, and you don't want to serve me no more."

It was a hazy, still, midsummer afternoon, and the little general store known as "Finny's" was as hot as an oven. Elizabeth Finny thought that the bread on the shelves would be double baked by the time anyone bothered to buy it; the colorful plastic bags it came wrapped in seemed to be blistering in the heat. By 10 AM, she had collected the boxes of chocolate candies and anything else that was prone to melting and moved it all into the big refrigerated cooler. By noontime, when a few bedraggled customers came around to buy their cold-lunch fixings, even the tin cans seemed to be drooping on the shelves. And an hour or so after that, the fly that had been buzzing around earlier in the day decided to give up and die on the glass top of the small meat counter, which was just as well. No one wanted to buy meat on such a sweltering day anyway. If it didn't spoil on the way home, it would just have to be cooked, and there wasn't a sane person in the county who wanted to light the oven or hear the sizzle of a fry pan on such a day. Elizabeth Finny had been selling cold pops and ice cream treats mostly. And not even that many of them. Business was as slow as the panting, old yellow hound that had taken up permanent residence in the blue shade of the store's tattered front awning.

"Elizabeth?"

If Molly Goodacre was feeling the heat, she didn't show it. She had on her stockings and good slip and leather shoes, the same as any other day and, yet, there wasn't a single drop of perspiration tickling her neck or plastering her wavy hair against her scalp. She had a pretty enough complexion that she wore no powder on her face, yet her nose and forehead showed no trace of an oily shine. The printed pattern on her old dress had faded into near obscurity from countless washings, but the dress itself still looked crisp from the ironing board, not tired and wilted. She made no move to fan herself and no particular effort to stand away from the sun that poured through the glass window of the rusted screen door. She simply seemed too intent upon speaking her piece to take any notice of the temperature at all.

"I'm here to apologize…and to explain," Molly said. She was clutching the strap of her handbag nervously. "And it ain't just because I want to buy some sugar for my porridge, though I do. It's because I'm ashamed. I never would have done such a thing if I hadn't been scared and alone, but I know God don't see that as a fit excuse. Don't suppose you do, either." Molly's eyes

glistened brightly as she spoke and it looked as though she might cry, but something in the determined set of her jaw guaranteed that she wouldn't.

Elizabeth, who sat primly on a stool behind the scarred counter, cleared her throat self-consciously but didn't bother to look up from her movie star magazine. She made no move, either, to add up the price of the few purchases that Molly had set next to the hulking old cash register. She ignored the little sack of sugar, tin of corned beef and box of wooden matches as intently as she ignored her customer.

Molly waited a minute or so for a response and then nodded, as if to accept that she would receive none.

"You're real angry and I don't blame you," she said, softly. "I expect that I would be, too, if I was in your shoes. But let me tell you how it happened, so you can understand. And so you can be careful, too. Because I'm sorry to say that you're not married to a very Christian man, Elizabeth. And I'm not just sayin' that because it's his word against mine."

Elizabeth frowned slightly and a thin, vertical line appeared between her well-groomed brows. She raised one slim, manicured hand to massage the tension away but gave no indication that she was listening to Molly at all.

"You know that since Hank died I been doing whatever I can to scrape together a living," Molly said. "I been sewing and taking in washing, and I clean houses whenever someone wants me to. But last winter was hard. It was hard for most everyone, what with the mill shut down and so many out of their jobs. Lots of people who used to have a bit of mending or laundry for me to do didn't have the money to pay me no more. So I got behind in my rent. And that's when your husband Tom came to see me.

"I was real surprised that first time, because he'd never come out to the house before. I always paid the rent to him right here at the store. You know that, Elizabeth, you took it from me more'n once. But he said that he'd come around to discuss 'the situation of my arrears,' as he put it. He wasn't in the door two minutes when he got all handsy on me."

Elizabeth Finny set her magazine down beside the register and crossed her arms over her small breasts. She refused to look at Molly, though; instead, she swiveled slightly on her stool so she could stare out the warped window that overlooked the dusty front road. Her lips were pressed together in a thin line.

"I want you to know," said Molly, "I didn't give in to him easy. I didn't give in to him at all that first time. All he got was a piece of my mind. But he kept comin' back, and then he told me that I was so far behind on my rent, he'd put me outdoors and sell all my things to make up for what he was owed. And the fight kinda went out of me then. I don't mind that I don't have much, Elizabeth, but I want to keep what I got. Especially those things that remind me of Hank. So I let him do what he wanted to do. And I have to say, I think that's about the highest rent anyone ever paid for three cold rooms and an outdoor privy.

"Afterwards, I said to him, 'Paid in full, then?' And he laughed in my face. Told me that I thought pretty highly of myself if I figured that one time would wipe out a debt of nearly $100. So he kept coming back. Every Sunday night. He told me that you liked to watch Ed Sullivan then, and he didn't care too much for it. You know, I liked that show too, and I've still got that little portable TV that Hank bought me for Christmas one year. But I never got to watch Mr. Sullivan anymore, not after your Tom started coming around. And it's funny, isn't it, the things that fill you up with resentment? I put up with him havin' his way with me for months and I just tried to put it out of my mind. But that television show—havin' to miss that every week just made me simmer.

"Finally, a few weeks back, I told him, 'There's a comedy act on Ed Sullivan that I'd like to watch tonight, so you'll have to wait.' And do you know what he did? He snapped the rabbit ears right off of my set. He just twisted 'em up and threw 'em in the corner and laughed about the whole thing. And that did it for me. I'd had enough. So I told Tom right then and there that if he didn't leave me be, I'd come talk to you. And he got in a rage then, that's for sure. But he must have known that I was tellin' the truth. And, so, I expect that he decided that he'd best tell you first. Tell you his version of the story, whatever that is. Because otherwise you wouldn't be givin' me such an awful cold shoulder."

Elizabeth stood up and turned her back on Molly completely. She began straightening the racks that were filled with chewing gum and cigarettes and other small items that were always sold from behind the counter.

Molly's lower lip quivered a little, and her eyes filled up. But she didn't cry. Instead, she took a deep breath, hung her purse over her arm primly and squared her shoulders.

"I'll come back to see you tomorrow, Elizabeth," she said. "After you've had some more time to think. And I'll keep coming back every day, if that's what it takes. I think you should know what kind of man you're married to. I need you to understand that I never meant to hurt your feelings none. And I'd like you to forgive me, because we been friends a long time and because I can't go walking all the way to town every time I need to buy a stick of butter."

Molly took one last, hurt look at Elizabeth's back and then walked out the store.

Elizabeth jumped and gave a little startled shriek.

"What is it?" Tom Finny walked out of the back rooms just as his wife cried out. He had been balancing the accounts, and his half-moon reading glasses were perched upon his nose. There was little ventilation in the storeroom that doubled as an office, and he had taken off his shirt hours earlier. The undershirt that he had kept on, only because Elizabeth insisted on a certain level of decency, had dark circles of perspiration showing beneath each arm and around his neck.

Elizabeth turned to face her husband. Her hand still rested on her chest, as if to calm her racing heart.

"The bell over the door rang again," she said. "Just like yesterday! There's been no one in or out of here for an hour; there's not a breeze to be found, but the bell rang just as if someone opened the door!"

"You've got heatstroke," Tom pronounced as he pulled an icy bottle of ginger ale out of the cooler for himself. "You should leave the door open anyhow. Move some air around."

"No, the flies come in," said Elizabeth. "And, anyway, I'm not feeling the heat. In fact…" she shivered and reached for the sweater that always hung on a hook behind the counter.

Tom nearly choked on his soda.

"You're wearing that sweater again?" He was incredulous. "It's 90 degrees in the shade today! Same as yesterday! And you're bundled up like Nanook of the North there!"

Elizabeth shrugged and hugged herself for warmth.

"I get chilled these days," she said. "One minute I'm sweltering hot, then the next I have gooseflesh all…" She stopped speaking abruptly and pointed to the counter by the cash register.

"Tom," she said, "did you put these here?" She was looking at the sugar, corned beef and matches.

"I just came out for a cold drink," he said. "It's your job to mind the store."

Elizabeth picked the items up and went about returning them to their proper places on the shelves. She did so
with her brow knit and her lips pursed.

Tom tipped the green glass bottle toward the ceiling
and drained the last of his ginger ale. He belched,
dropped the bottle into a wooden crate that sat next to
the cooler and started off toward the back.

"You know, it's so strange here lately. Strange things
happening, and business is so bad," said Elizabeth in a
thoughtful tone.

Tom paused in the doorway.

"It's the heat," he said. "People are staying home under
their shade trees."

Elizabeth carried on as though she hadn't heard him.

"And Molly Goodacre is on my mind so much these
days," she said.

"That deadbeat?" replied Tom. "Ran off without paying her back rent."

Elizabeth snapped back to attention.

"That poor woman is as honest as the day is long and
you know it, Tom Finny!" she declared. "She's bound to
show up with your money."

"I wouldn't bet on it," he grunted. "I shouldn't have let
her owe me so long. I'm too good to people, that's my
problem."

Elizabeth didn't comment, but one of her eyebrows
arched in a subtly cynical expression.

"When someone disappears like that, you can bet
they've got terrible troubles," she said. "I just hope she's
all right."

"There's some good news, though," said Tom. "I think
I got her place rented. A spinster gal who works over at

the post office was looking at it. She doesn't have a lot of money, but I think we can work something out."

"It's premature, Tom," said Elizabeth. "Molly will be back."

It was all that Elizabeth said, and she didn't mean for it to sound threatening, but Tom felt the ginger ale in his stomach lurch a little.

I just downed that drink too fast, and it's so bloody hot in here, he told himself. But he knew that it was his wife's comment—"Molly will be back"—that had unsettled him so.

The Goodacre woman wouldn't be back. He had made damn sure of it after she had threatened to tell his wife about his method of collecting back rent. He had come at her from behind; she didn't see it coming and probably never knew what hit her. It was the television set, the one that had caused all the problems in the first place. Tom had hoisted it up like a trophy and brought it down...

So she wasn't coming back, and everything was fine. Tom knew that as he wiped his greasy forehead and picked up his pen and went back to work balancing the accounts.

But, still, he felt uneasy.

Still.

And, suddenly, strangely, in the midst of the scorching heat, Tom Finny found himself wishing for a sweater.

"My mom always tells me that she'd KILL me if she caught me hitchhiking. But then I heard her telling her friend about this one time that SHE did…"

A Lift To The Train

Kathy Tate woke up early on the morning that she was planning to run away from home. She slipped silently into a pair of jeans and a sweatshirt, tied the laces of her canvas tennis shoes and stuffed the $37.50 that she had saved into her pocket—more than enough to buy a train ticket to the city. She had checked into it the same day she had secretly packed a bag with her favorite possessions and hidden it beneath her bed.

She left by the back door, the one that didn't creak, in the chilly dark hour before dawn. Then she lugged her bag down the long driveway to the gravel road and down the gravel road to the highway. Once she reached the highway, Kathy sat down on her suitcase and hoped that there would be some traffic before the sun came up. Her best bet was to be on the train before anyone noticed that she was missing.

She had been waiting for 15 minutes—long enough that she was wondering whether she would have to abandon her mission until the next day—when she heard the drone of a motor in the distance. A set of headlights crested the hill and Kathy's stomach clenched. She stood up, stuck out her thumb and prayed that the car didn't belong to one of the neighbors. If someone she knew stopped to pick her up, she would be in a huge jam. But as the car slowed and pulled over to the shoulder, Kathy noted with relief that it wasn't a bit familiar.

In fact, it was downright strange.

It was an older model, with speckles of rust and a paint job that was way past its prime. Perhaps in an effort to dress the car up, the owner had gotten overly enthusiastic with bumper stickers, putting them in places that could not, by any stretch of the imagination, be mistaken for a bumper. When Kathy got closer to the car, she could see that the no-holds-barred approach to auto decoration had been taken to the interior as well. A string of little pom-poms—her father called them "dingle balls"— had been strung around the roof liner like Christmas lights. And every inch of the dashboard was being used to display an assortment of whimsical, cheap, plastic toys.

For the first time since she had formed her plan, Kathy felt uncertain. She had never considered what she might do if a crazy person pulled over to give her a ride. In her fantasy, the driver had always been someone normal and sane who was completely sympathetic to her plight.

A scrawny hand reached over and pushed open the passenger-side door. The eerie, pale, interior light flickered on. Kathy hesitantly bent over and looked into the vehicle. A woman with a wild-looking perm and a lot of costume jewelry smiled at her from across the front seat.

"C'mon, honey!" she said. "Time's a-wastin'!"

Kathy thought of hauling her heavy bag all the way back to the house and having to hide it until another opportunity arose. She looked at the woman again. She was a little weird—fashion challenged, definitely—but she appeared to be harmless enough. Eccentric, probably, but not crazy. Kathy came to a decision. She got in the car.

"Where you going, honey?" the woman asked as she pulled back out on the highway.

Kathy smiled. She had been dreaming for weeks about having this conversation with someone.

"If you could give me a lift to the train station in town, I'd sure appreciate it," she said. Then, recklessly, because she had been bottling the secret for so long, she blurted out, "I'm going to live in the city."

"The city! My, my!" the woman seemed to be impressed. Kathy was beginning to like her, despite her bizarre hair and collection of dime-store accessories. She could sense that this woman, unlike her uptight parents, was taking her very seriously.

"Yeah," said Kathy. "I'm going to get a job and an apartment. Then I'm going to write novels and become famous. I could never do it here. I'm too repressed here." *Repressed* was her new favorite word, and she used it often.

"Oh, I understand."

There it was. Someone understood. The woman offered no lectures, no judgment, no advice about staying in school and getting good grades. Kathy had long suspected that her parents were rigid fascists. That the first person she met on her journey to the outside world should provide her with such a stark contrast proved to her that she was right in trying to escape them.

"Are you from around here?" Kathy asked, trying to make adult-sounding conversation.

"Used to be," said the woman. "But now I'm not really from anywhere. I just travel around. Spend most of my time right here in this car."

Kathy looked around the vehicle. There were piles of clothes draped over the back seat, and the smell of stale food hung in the air. A picture of a German shepherd, set in a blue plastic frame, had been attached to the glove box with a piece of wire.

"You *live* in the car?" she asked.

"Sure, why not? The price is right, and I'm not stuck anyplace I don't like. Kind of like you."

Kathy frowned.

"How like me?" she asked.

"You know," the woman said, with a bright, knowing smile. "Free. You and I are part of a rare breed. We're not tied down to anything or anyone. Thirty years ago, I was just like you, and I've never stopped moving. I'm livin' a dream!"

Kathy smiled politely but said nothing. She stared out the window at the sun that was pushing up over the horizon and wondered how the poor woman could possibly see her life as a dream. Kathy's dream involved making a lot of money and owning a fancy car that she didn't have to live in. It involved great success, so she could prove to everyone how misunderstood and underestimated she had always been. It did *not* involve a bad perm and a smelly old car and a lot of plastic hula girls and a tacky key chain with a rabbit's foot and a big, gaudy, gold tag with the initials…

"Hey!" said Kathy when she noticed the tag dangling from the key in the ignition. "Those are my initials! 'K.T.' Kathy Tate. What do yours stand for?"

"Everybody just calls me 'K.T.'" said the woman. "I mean, they *would*, if I had anybody around to call me anything!" She laughed at that, as though it wasn't pathetically sad.

Kathy shifted her suitcase on her lap, trying to get more comfortable.

"You must have friends," she said. "You must have somebody."

The woman named K.T. shook her fuzzy head.

"Not really," she said. "Not anymore. I guess I gave up my family when I struck out on my own. As for friends, I think a person mostly collects them in school. Maybe at work. And my life's never been like that, you know? I've been on the road, having adventures."

"When you started out, is this what you wanted?" asked Kathy. "I mean—is this how you thought things would be?" She squirmed again in her seat. The suitcase seemed to be getting heavier by the minute. It was cutting off the circulation to her legs.

K.T. laughed.

"No, this isn't what I pictured in my head," she admitted. "I thought things would be a little grander. I had big ideas. I was going to be a somebody! But it turned out that I wasn't as successful as you're planning to be. I should have gotten more schooling, I guess. Should have stuck with my folks. I'm just talking about myself, of

course. But it was hard to find any success when I spent all my time just staying alive, if you know what I mean."

The sun had climbed higher, painting the sky pink and gold with its rays. Kathy was suddenly homesick for her bedroom, for the way the light of dawn looked when it was filtered through her gauzy white curtains.

"Do you think I should go back?" she said. It had been a long time since she had asked someone's opinion. Generally, other people's opinions of her life made her feel *repressed*.

"I don't know," said K.T. "You have to figure that out. But I'll tell you one thing: If you go down this road much farther, you'll have to keep going. Comes a time when heading back just doesn't feel like an option anymore."

Kathy chewed thoughtfully on her lip. An hour earlier, she had been so certain...

"I'll take you to the train if you want," K.T. said, interrupting Kathy's reverie. "But you might want to consider that there'll be other trains. Trains that will take you farther."

She said nothing more. Kathy sat there with her heavy bag digging into her thighs, listening to the jingle of K.T.'s cheap bracelets, staring at her menagerie of sun-bleached plastic companions. Finally, she spoke.

"Can you let me out, please?" she said. "I think I'd better go home."

K.T. winked at her and pulled over to the side of the road. She braked quickly, causing the dingle balls and hula girls to sway with wild abandon.

"You're a smart kid," she said, "and you'll do good. Just be patient, hey?"

Kathy nodded and thanked her for the ride. She opened the door of the car and climbed out, dragging her suitcase behind her. Then she swung the door shut…

…and the sky went black.

It happened that fast. One moment, she was wondering how long it would take her to hitchhike back to the farm, and the next, the sun was gone. It had dropped back behind the horizon like a stone. It took awhile for Kathy to realize that K.T.'s car had vanished too, and even longer for her to notice that the landscape itself had changed. When her eyes finally adjusted to the gloom, she saw that she was standing at the familiar intersection of the highway and the gravel road near her home. She could tell by the faint glow on the horizon and the dewy fragrance in the air that it was still before dawn. In the distance, she could see a tiny pinpoint of light. She knew it was the naked bulb that hung over her own back porch.

Kathy had never been so relieved or so afraid in her whole life. All she wanted, suddenly, was to make it back to the safety of that little porch light. So, on shaky legs, she began to walk. She walked quickly, as quickly as a girl carrying her life in a heavy suitcase could go. When she was halfway up the road to the house, she heard a vehicle out on the highway. She didn't turn to look. She was afraid that it would be a crazy-looking old car, plastered with bumper stickers, coming to give her a lift to the train.

Kathy managed to sneak in the back door before the sun rose. Her parents never knew that she had been gone. She tiptoed upstairs, lugging her heavy case. When she got to her room she unpacked it, knowing that she wouldn't be needing it after all.

Her clothes went back into drawers. Her toiletries went back on her dresser. She put her shoes on the floor of the closet and slid her favorite books back into their places on her shelf. The suitcase was empty then—or, at least, it should have been. But as Kathy begin to zip it closed, she noticed a bit of gaudy plastic, the size of an egg, sliding around on the nylon lining at the bottom. She reached in and pulled the item out.

It was a key tag. A gold spray-painted one. With her initials on it—"K.T."

She sat on the floor for a while, holding the tag in her hand and wondering how it had come to be in the bottom of her bag. Finally, when she was too tired to wonder any more, she got up and put the plastic tag in her keepsake box. It seemed important to keep it, although she wasn't sure why. She knew that she would never see K.T. again.

Kathy was wrong about that.

She did see her again. And, as the years passed, she saw her more and more frequently. Sometimes she would pass by a store window and happen to catch a glimpse of K.T. peering out of the glass. Sometimes she would see her image in an unflattering photograph. By the time Kathy was in her 40s, she could look into the mirror whenever she wanted, imagine a bad perm and tacky jewelry and the kind of weathered look that came from living a hard life, and she would see K.T. staring out at her. And, even though she had stayed in school and been patient and done all the right things, it was still good to have that reminder. Every time she needed to choose between something fast and something worthwhile, she would look into the mirror and hold the plastic key tag and ask herself:

"Which train will take me farther?"

The answer was always the same. K.T., that woman of remarkable vision, always helped her to remember.

"We're always talking about ghosts like they're disembodied spirits, you know? But what if they were something else? My friend used to say that there were ghosts inside her head...Maybe there are a lot of people who feel that way..."

So Familiar

Norma looked at her pale, mottled reflection in the fitting room mirror and tried in vain to squish her doughy roll of stomach fat someplace where it couldn't be seen. But no such place existed. "Try the tankini," the size-two sales girl had urged her. "It's a good style for hiding figure flaws." Norma's figure, however, had the kind of flaws that came from 20 depressing years of sitting on the couch binging on cookies, and it wasn't going to be disguised by a few ounces of Lycra, no matter how well designed they might be.

She tried sucking in her gut, but that only served to give the fat a sort of puckered appearance. Norma let out her breath with a *whoosh* and gave up trying.

Why am I doing this to myself? she wondered. *I'll never go to the pool anyway.* Earlier in the week, she had been considering an aquasize class. Two minutes in front of the fun-house mirror, bathed in harsh fluorescent lights, modeling the $85 tankini had dealt soundly with that small ambition, though. Norma thought that she would get herself a little consolation treat from the bakery and maybe rent a video...

That was when she saw Shelley Cooper.

Norma hadn't seen Shelley for decades, not since high school, when the popular girl had seemingly dedicated her own life to ruining Norma's. There was no mistaking her, though. She still had the same glossy, pale blonde hair and it still framed her model-perfect face in buoyant layers. Her wide, green eyes still held an icy look, and her pink lips still curled in a defiant sneer. Her legs were every bit as long as Norma remembered, and her stride was every bit as purposeful and confident.

She was striding across the room toward Norma.

Norma ducked her head down instinctively. Her right hand came up to the side of her head, as if to shade her eyes. Suddenly, she was more concerned about hiding her face than she was about hiding her stomach. It would have been horrible to bump into Shelley Cooper anywhere, at any time, but half-naked, in a fitting room, without a speck of makeup, during a bad hair day? It was unthinkable. Norma kept her eyes down and tried to make a dash for the curtained cubicle where she had left her clothes.

"How fat!"

It amazed Norma that, even after so many years, one of Shelley's insults could cut just as deeply. She felt her cheeks reddening, and the corners of her eyes began to prickle with tears.

"Ma'am? I said 'How's that?'" It was the twiggy sales clerk.

Norma turned around cautiously and looked at the girl. She was blonde and leggy and pretty—but her resemblance to the terrible Shelley Cooper ended there. Also, she was clearly no more than 20 or 21 years old. That Norma could have mistaken her for someone who would be in her 40s was ridiculous.

"Finished, cow?" sneered the clerk.

Norma blinked in disbelief. "Cow" had been Shelley's pet name for her.

"I beg your pardon?" she gasped.

The girl blinked back. She was beginning to look as confused as Norma felt.

"I just asked if you were finished now," she repeated. "I can bring you some other suits, if you like. We have a great one-piece with a bit of a skirt at the bottom. It's super for hiding the hips."

"No thanks. I'm done," said Norma. She stepped into the cubicle and rudely yanked the curtain shut.

Five minutes later, Norma had left the store and was walking down the mall. For some reason that she couldn't quite identify, she was still upset. She hadn't really run into her old high-school nemesis, but she felt every bit as humiliated as if she had. It was unsettling.

It was the whole swimsuit thing, she thought to herself. *Very bad for the emotional well-being.* That and the fact that the sales girl had looked so familiar. Norma imagined the jumbled circuits in her brain putting together a familiar image with a familiar feeling and producing a full-blown, panic-inducing hallucination. A hallucination with flippy blonde tresses and mean green eyes just like that woman at the information kiosk…

Norma sucked her breath in sharply and performed a stage-worthy double take. The sales clerk hadn't been Shelley Cooper, but this woman most certainly was and she was staring at Norma with an expression of absolute recognition. Suddenly, Norma realized that what she had experienced in the fitting room had been a warning, a premonition that she was about to encounter the worst person from her past.

"Can I help you?" The woman at the kiosk counter raised her eyebrows in a bored way as she spoke. Norma realized then that she had been staring stupidly at her; she was literally slack-jawed. And why? The woman was a brunette. Her eyes might have been green, but it was difficult to tell, the way they swam behind a thick pair of corrective lenses.

"Lady, do you have a question or something?"

Norma didn't bother to answer. She put her head down and quickly strode past the sign that advertised *Information! Change! Parking Validation!* She managed to make it to the end of the mall without making eye contact with another person. When she was going through the revolving exit door, she noticed that the woman on the opposite side was wearing a pair of white leather boots identical to the ones Shelley had often used to trip Norma in the school halls. But it couldn't possibly have been Shelley. It couldn't have been the same boots. That's what Norma told herself, but she refused to raise her eyes all the same.

The Number 32 bus that ran between the mall and the street where Norma lived was nearly full that afternoon. She was forced to take a seat near the back, just in front of a boisterous group of teenagers. She listened to their snickering for the entire ride and knew instinctively that it was directed at her.

The next morning, when Norma arrived at work, she was shocked to see that Karen, the woman who sat at the desk opposite her own, was sporting a new hairstyle. It wasn't the change that alarmed Norma—Karen tended to be adventurous with her hair and frequently began the week with a new cut or color. It was her choice of style that was so disconcerting: Karen had gone blonde—pale blonde—with flippy long layers.

"What made you do that?" Norma asked her. There was a bit of an accusing tone in her voice and she was frowning as she examined her office-mate's appearance.

"What made you notice all of a sudden?" Karen shot back. "I had this done weeks ago."

Norma didn't believe her but couldn't think of a good reason why she might lie. For the rest of the day, she found it difficult to concentrate on her work. She kept glancing sneakily over the top of her computer screen at her newly coiffed coworker, looking for some evidence that her hairdo was a recent change. Finally, she decided to simply ask someone.

"Maeve," she said in a low voice to the sales secretary who came to deposit a pile of paperwork on her desk, "how long has Karen worn her hair that way?"

"Cow! Should I know?" spat Maeve as she threw down her papers.

Norma was stunned.

"*What* did you say to me?" she finally stammered.

Maeve looked at her innocently.

"I said 'How should I know?'" she shrugged. "I've got enough to keep track of without making it my business to note changing hairstyles."

That evening, Norma curled up on the couch with her Persian cat, Twinkle. She ate a huge bowl of buttered popcorn while she watched one of her favorite TV shows. It amazed her that she had never before noticed how much the cast looked like Shelley Cooper's smirking crowd of high-school friends. It was disturbing how often the actors seemed to be looking slyly out of the television, directly at her. They were smiling, always smiling, but there was nothing friendly in their expressions at all.

"So you're feeling a little anxious these days?" said the doctor.

Norma nodded tensely.

"Yes, very," she said. "Very anxious. And I'm having trouble sleeping."

The doctor looked up from her file and squinted at her over the wire frame of his eyeglasses. Norma knew that he was assessing the dark hollows hanging beneath her eyes. It had been three weeks since she had begun to see Shelley Cooper everywhere; it had been two weeks since the teenaged witch had invaded her dreams. Norma had since found herself in an impossible situation. She could sleep and suffer the nightmares of being back in high school, tormented by Shelley, or she could keep herself awake by watching infomercials that appeared to star Shelley and seemed to be directed specifically at her.

Look at all that blubber, Cow! You can live with it or you can lose it, with my "Fat-Blaster-9000!" Not that a stupid, lazy bovine like you would ever actually get around to calling 1-800...

"And how's your appetite?" the doctor was asking.

"A little too good," replied Norma. It was an understatement. There had been a lot of ice-cream therapy happening. She squirmed guiltily in her chair and felt the elastic waistband of her skirt binding.

"Well," droned the doctor, "overeating can be a sign of depression, too." He gave her a prescription and a standard warning to be cautious about the dosage and told her to come back in a month.

"And, in the meantime," he added, "you should try to get out more. Don't isolate yourself; it just tends to worsen the condition."

Get out more. Norma didn't know whether to laugh or cry. She left her apartment only when it was absolutely necessary. It was torturous to go out and encounter Shelley Cooper at every turn. Shelley was at the grocery story; Shelley was at the post office; Shelley was even at the doctor's office. Bearing that in mind, Norma kept her eyes focused on the carpet as she walked past the nurse's desk.

"Take care," called the nurse in her friendly, bell-like voice. But Norma had seen her on the way in; she had seen the hair and the eyes and the permanent smirk and she refused to face her again. She got on the elevator and stared at her shoes until the big metal door slid closed.

▴▴▴

"Don't be stupid enough to take these on an empty stomach, you fat, freaking cow," said the pharmacist.

Norma nodded but would not look at the woman's face. The prescription was handed across the counter in its crisp little white bag. The perfectly manicured hand holding it wore a ring with the crest of Norma's high school.

There were a dozen people waiting at the bus stop. Every one of them—including the newborn strapped to its mother in a carrier and the old, black man with the deeply lined face—had a light blonde, layered flip and mean, green eyes. Norma took one look at the group and decided to walk the 23 blocks to her apartment.

She started taking some of the pills along the way, reasoning that, with all she ate, her stomach was probably never *really* empty anyway.

She slept that night. It was a heavy, drug-soaked sleep from which she woke late, feeling groggy and ill. She called the office and spoke to the Shelley-clone receptionist.

"I'm not feeling well," she said. "I won't be in today."

"What's the matter?" taunted the voice on the phone. "Can't find anything big enough to wear?"

Norma didn't answer. Instead, she calmly placed the phone in its cradle and asked in a flat voice, "How was that?"

"That'll do, Cow," purred Twinkle with a toss of her perfectly groomed blonde coat. Then she narrowed her emerald eyes until they were two mean little slits and said, "Now, let's get those pills out here."

It was four days before anyone at the office began to wonder if Norma was ever coming back in. It was a full week before the caretaker of her apartment building used his master key to open her suite. The vague smell that the neighbors had been complaining about exploded into an overwhelming stench the moment the door swung open. The man held his handkerchief over his mouth and nose as he went from room to room, looking for the source of the odor. When he found it, he vomited on his shoes and then called the police.

Even after the body was removed, the tall cop hung around. He kept asking questions that made the caretaker feel stupid and useless. "I don't know" and "I'm not sure" seemed to be the only answers he had. But, then, why was he *expected* to know so much about Norma Bennett? She had only been a tenant. He had over 100 tenants in the two buildings that he looked after. None of them had ever up and died on him before.

Eventually, after what felt like forever, the cop appeared to be finished. He was looking over his notes, tapping the paper thoughtfully with his pen. It was then that the caretaker decided to ask a question of his own.

"Say, you don't think that, well, you know…is there anything for us to worry about?" He cleared his throat nervously as he waited for an answer.

"What do you mean?" the cop looked down at him with an irritated frown.

"Well," the caretaker struggled to rephrase his question, "was it catching, do you suppose? Did she die of anything contagious?"

The cop, who had sealed the empty prescription bottle in an evidence bag and watched the coroner lift the bloated corpse out of a crusty sheet of dried puke, began to laugh.

"I doubt it," he said in a condescending tone. "I *seriously* doubt it."

Hours later, when he was all alone, the caretaker still felt idiotic and small and intimidated. There was something uncomfortably familiar about the feeling, and there had been something equally familiar about the cop...

Wagner's Gas and Auto Repair, 1976, his memory finally informed him. That was it. The caretaker felt the great relief that came with unearthing a stubbornly buried memory.

"Dan Wagner," he said to himself. "The damn cop looked just like Dan Wagner!"

Dan Wagner had been the bully of a boss who had fired him from his first job. The cop had had the same towering height, broad shoulders and loud, mocking voice. It was little wonder that he had felt so ineffectual in the man's presence.

The caretaker hadn't thought about his old boss in a very long time. But he knew that if he was to see Dan Wagner swaggering down the street in the future, he would recognize him in an instant.

The cop had made the memory fresh again.

It had been lying dormant, but it had come back and now it was all so familiar…

"My older cousin rented this place once that was haunted—I swear! All this really weird stuff used to go on…"

The Presence

The agent was about ready to close his office for the day when one of his clients, who looked angry and upset and hadn't bothered to make an appointment, burst in.

"I need to speak with you," the client insisted, "about that house. That horrible house that you rented to me!"

The agent sighed. It was no way to end the day, having to deal with a sticky problem. The sight of the client, flushed and flustered, made him wish that he had locked the door and turned out the lights five minutes earlier than usual. But he hadn't. So the client was in his office and would have to be dealt with. The agent motioned to a chair on the opposite side of his desk and invited him to sit.

"Bernard, please," he said. "Tell me what's wrong."

He was trying to show concern, trying to soothe his client. But the innocent query only served to enrage the man.

"What's wrong?" he shrieked in his prissy way. "*What's wrong?* Everything is wrong, thanks to you and your deceptive way of doing business! You know all about what goes on in that house! You *must* know! And yet you let me move in without a word of warning!"

"I assure you that I would never knowingly…"

"Oh, really?" hissed the client, through clenched teeth. "Then why is it that you didn't move in there yourself? Such a big, beautiful house. Vacant, you said. And such a bargain! Tell me why you didn't want to take advantage of such a bargain?"

The agent squirmed in his seat.

"Just tell me what's happened," he said. "I'm sure there's something that can be done."

There was a degree of sincerity in the agent's voice. The client heard it and was disarmed. For the first time since he had stormed into the office, his rage took a back seat to his despair.

"That's the problem, though," the client said. "I don't think there's anything that anyone can do. And it's terrible, truly. I've seen things…"

The client buried his face in his hands. The agent wasn't sure if he was weeping and didn't wish to embarrass him by asking. But he quietly, discreetly moved the tissue box that sat on his desk nearer to the edge by which the client sat.

"When did it begin?" he asked after a few moments had passed.

The client took a deep breath and leaned back in his chair. The agent noticed the shadows beneath his eyes then and the pallor of his complexion.

"I first noticed something wrong about a month ago," he said. "It was days—certainly no more than a few days after I moved in. Do you remember that

magnificent thunderstorm that we had? It knocked the power out."

"I do remember," said the agent.

"Well," the client continued, "I do so enjoy a lovely storm. And after the lights went out it was even better. Much more dramatic. So I was sitting in my easy chair, watching the lightning through the big picture window when…When…"

"Go on," urged the agent.

The client began to speak more dramatically.

"Suddenly, there were lights everywhere!" he said. "Spots of light, flaring up like candle flames, all over the house. I didn't know what to make of it; it seemed impossible. I stood up. I was turning this way and that way—every time I saw a new light flash in the periphery of my vision, I would spin around to see what was causing it. My heart was pounding, I can tell you. And then, suddenly...I sensed a presence behind me. So I turned, slowly, and there it was. This face."

The client shuddered at the recollection.

"What sort of face?" the agent asked after several seconds.

The client squeezed his eyes shut.

"The most terrible face," he said. "So fleshy and florid. And vacuous. It looked right through me with these empty, unseeing eyes, as though I was not even there. I can tell you, that's an experience that you never want to have. It chilled me thoroughly to see those eyes."

"What happened next?" From a businessman's point of view, the agent didn't want there to be any more. He was already imagining the value of his property depreciating, particularly if word spread. But he was drawn into a fascinating story as easily as anyone, and he wanted to know what happened. "Tell me," he urged.

"The lights came back on," said the client. "The electricity, I mean. The other lights—the eerie, flickering flames—went out then, one by one. It was really quite disconcerting."

The agent's mood lifted.

"So that was it, then?" he asked. He was thinking that, if nothing else had happened, the client might be convinced to stay. He might be convinced that his imagination had been working overtime in unfamiliar surroundings...

The client interrupted the agent's hopeful reverie.

"I wish that had been 'it,' as you say. I wish it all the time. But that was only the beginning of my frightening ordeal."

The agent pressed his fingers wearily against his temples.

"Then go on," he said.

The client shook his head and held out his hands in a frustration.

"I can hardly begin to tell it all," he said. "The noises! The horrible noises that I have had to put up with. Constant chattering and music—the most dreadful music I have ever heard, blaring out suddenly at all hours of the day and night. The television comes on, too, very unexpectedly and during the most offensive programs."

"Have you tried unplugging it?"

The client seemed to take offense.

"I can assure you that I have tried all sensible solutions," he snapped. "And I can also tell you that they have accomplished nothing, other than to aggravate the situation. Every one of my efforts resulted in hours of slamming doors and frantic, yammering voices."

"And the voices," the agent spoke slowly and carefully. "Can you understand what they're saying?"

The client's posture stiffened.

"Only recently," he said. "They've become more clear. Nearer, it seems. I can understand a word here and there and I dare say that they are planning to drive me out. Of my own home—can you believe it? They plan to drive me out!"

The agent looked thoughtful.

"And do you plan to let them?" he asked.

The client was appalled.

"What choice have I?" he stammered.

"You could stay," the agent suggested mildly. "Have some fun with it."

"*Fun?* I'm afraid!"

"They're probably afraid of you!"

"Why on earth would they fear me?"

The agent laughed despite himself.

"Bernard!" he said. "You're a GHOST!"

The client frowned and turned away.

"I prefer 'ethereal entity,' if you don't mind," he sniffed. "And it doesn't mean that I'm interested in common haunting. That's why I requested a vacant house, not one filled with wild, terrifying, unattractive living beings."

"Okay, okay," the agent held up his hands, signaling his surrender. "I'll be honest; I was hoping you wouldn't notice them. Not everyone does, you know. And I didn't exactly have a vacant vacancy the day you came in..."

"I knew it!"

"But I do now, so let me make it up to you—what do you say? Two months of free rent in a new place—to compensate you for any inconvenience you may have suffered."

"Terror is what it was," the client pouted. "I thought I was losing my mind!"

The agent said nothing more. The silence drew out, but he did not break it, which had always been his way of saying that the final offer was on the table. Finally, the client took a deep breath and raised one hand in a fluttery gesture seemingly meant to wave any remaining unpleasantness away.

"Oh, fine," he said. "What's this other house, then? The truly vacant one?"

The agent told him about it: a fine, decrepit bit of abandoned beach property with broken windows and no plumbing. Utterly uninhabitable by the living.

"That does sound nice," breathed the client. "And I could use a restful time at the shore after all I've been through."

So a deal was struck and the client left happy.

But the agent looked at the clock and sighed.

He was half an hour late for the party. The woman whose home he haunted was hosting a dinner for some coworkers. He had been planning, for weeks, to attend. He thought he might levitate the cat, give them something worthwhile to discuss around the water cooler the next day. But now he would have to rush and he never did his best work when he was rushed...

"Oh, don't be silly," he muttered to himself. "Let them enjoy their meal. Float Fluffy around after the coffee is served." Unlike some of his clients, he enjoyed haunting and sometimes had to stop himself from being too much of a perfectionist.

And, as for the house, the place with the troublesome, boisterous family...

The agent smiled suddenly. He had just the ghost. A tough old spectral spinster named Rebecca who had died so long ago that she had only distant, faded, watercolor memories of her earthly body. She didn't even believe in the living, she had told him once, which would make her the perfect placement.

The agent was smiling to himself and humming as he locked the door, turned out the lights and flipped the sign in the window to read "closed." He was feeling good. Really good.

That's the best way to end the day, he thought as he drifted on down the street. *By solving a really sticky problem.*

"My cousin says that there's a ghost who's visited her since she was in the first grade. She feels like she knows him. She even has a name for him…"

Brenda's Buddy

Brenda O'Connell believed in ghosts all her life. She had been seeing one since the day she turned six. On that day, after the party and the gifts and the cake and the fun, her mother had asked her to sit down for a cuddle in the big rocking chair. Brenda happily crawled up on her mother's lap and nestled her face against the soft, perfumed hollow beneath her chin. They gently rocked back and forth. Brenda's mother asked her how she had liked her party and what had been her favorite gift. Then, after a time, she grew very serious.

"You're getting to be a big girl, Brenda," she said. "Big enough to know important things." And then she asked Brenda if she knew what the word "adoption" meant.

Brenda wasn't sure, so her mother explained it to her. And then she explained that Brenda had been adopted when she was just a tiny, wriggling baby wrapped in a pink flannel blanket.

"We chose you," said Mrs. O'Connell, "which made you our baby girl, just the same as if I had given birth to you myself." Then she asked Brenda if she felt confused or upset about anything, or if there was anything that she wanted to say.

Brenda furrowed her brow and pursed her lips and thought about it.

"No," she finally said. "I can't see that it makes anything different. You're still my mom and Daddy is still my dad and I'm still me."

Her mother was pleased.

"You have it exactly right, Brenda," she said. Silently, she thanked God for sending her a child who was so unflappable.

Brenda did tend to be calm and sensible for a child so young. They were qualities that stood her in good stead that night after she was tucked into her bed. For after the light was turned out and the door was shut, a glowing apparition appeared in her bedroom.

It was a man—a handsome young man with wavy, dark hair and kind eyes. He was smiling down at Brenda in such a benevolent fashion that she knew instinctively there was no need to be afraid. Quite the opposite, she offered him a welcoming smile of her own and lifted her small hand off the pillow in a little wave. The young man smiled even more broadly at this, and his eyes shined all the more brightly. Then he vanished as though someone had turned off a switch.

"Good-bye," Brenda said sleepily. Then she closed her eyes, thinking that all in all, it had been a very eventful day.

Brenda was in no way a secretive child, so the next morning, she told her parents about her spectral visitor. They listened to her attentively while casting one another the occasional meaningful, sidelong glance. Later, they discussed it when they were alone.

"What's the harm?" said Mr. O'Connell, who was an open-minded man.

"Exactly," said his equally open-minded wife.

They concluded that the visitor was either an angel or a figment of Brenda's young imagination, and that neither one would do her any harm.

In this accepting atmosphere, Brenda felt free to talk about the apparition. Every time he paid her a visit—and his visits were frequent thereafter—she would mention it to her parents. Before long, the three of them had named him. He was always referred to as "Brenda's Buddy."

"I saw my Buddy last night," Brenda would announce as she poured cream on her oatmeal. Or, in the evening, she would report, "Buddy came to watch me on the monkey bars today." For, after the first few times she saw him in her darkened bedroom, it seemed that Brenda could see the ghost anywhere.

Brenda's Buddy showed up in the schoolyard, smiling warmly as he leaned against the fence and watched her playing with her friends. He was there at every birthday party that she could remember after her sixth, and even came to collect her from a friend's birthday party once. Brenda had been waiting at the front door of her friend's house when she saw her father coming up the paved walk. Right behind him, at his elbow, was the shimmering apparition of her Buddy. His image winked out of sight just as Mr. O'Connell stepped up on the front porch.

"Dad," Brenda told her father, "Buddy was walking with you just now!"

"Is that so?" said Mr. O'Connell. Later, he told Brenda's mother that he had felt an odd buzzing, like static electricity, tickling one side of his body as he approached the house.

"So maybe there's something to it," he mused.

"Maybe," said his wife. She had often thought that a girl as levelheaded as their Brenda would be unlikely to maintain such an elaborate fantasy for such a long time.

The years went by and Brenda grew, and her Buddy watched her every step of the way. His smiling, glowing form once appeared to her backstage following her performance in the school play. She awoke one Christmas morning to see him sitting on the edge of her bed, gazing lovingly down at her. And, every time her Buddy appeared, Brenda felt as if she had been wrapped in a warm blanket of encouragement and love.

"I hope you're always with me," Brenda whispered to him once when she was feeling quite emotional. Her Buddy, who never spoke, had placed one glowing hand over his heart to show that he would be.

Brenda was not the rebellious type, so her parents had a relatively easy time of it during her teenage years. The older she grew, however, the more curious she became regarding the circumstances of her adoption. She would look in the mirror and wonder who had given her such dark eyes and such stubbornly curly hair. She asked many questions, and her parents answered those that they could. But they couldn't tell her everything because they didn't know everything. One day—a day that Mr. and Mrs. O'Connell had always considered to be an inevitability—Brenda made an announcement.

"You will always be my mother and father," she said, "but I'd like to know more about my biological parents. I'd like you to help me find them."

Brenda's parents agreed that they would. They hired an agency that specialized in such things and, within a year, Brenda was handed an envelope. Inside was a piece of paper with a name, address and phone number—the identity of her birth mother.

🦇

"I'm nervous," Brenda said to her mother the day they drove to the address that the agency had given them. "What if she doesn't like me?"

Brenda's mother scoffed at the idea.

"She was very pleasant with you on the phone, wasn't she?" she said. "And besides, what's not to like? You're a wonderful girl, Brenda. She should be delighted to meet you."

Brenda appreciated her mother's encouragement, but butterflies still fluttered madly in her stomach.

She didn't want me then—she may not want any part of me now was what she couldn't stop herself from thinking.

The nervousness stayed with her as she stepped out of the car and waved good-bye to her mother. It persisted as she slowly walked up the path that led to a modest brick house sheltered by great, leafy trees. It was so terrible that Brenda thought she might lose her nerve altogether and go back out to the road to wait for her mother—her *real* mother—to pick her up. But then, as she stood at the front door considering whether to ring the bell or run, she saw something that changed her mind.

A warm light coming from the far end of the veranda caught her attention. She looked and saw that it was her Buddy. He was perched comfortably on the railing, glowing more radiantly than ever, and he was looking at Brenda with tremendous love. He tilted his head playfully to one side and made a nodding gesture in the direction of the door.

She knew then that it would be all right. The butterflies grew quiet and she rang the bell.

Brenda's birth mother, though emotional, was very happy to see her. The visit went extremely well. Brenda learned that, when she was born, her birth parents had been teenagers, ill-equipped to handle the responsibility of caring for a newborn infant.

"It's a common story, I know," the woman said as she served Brenda tea and cake. "Nothing surprising or glamorous. But if it helps you to know it, your biological father and I were very much in love. We did marry, in fact, a couple of years after you were born."

"And are you still together?" Brenda asked hopefully. It seemed impossibly romantic to her that her birth parents might still be as happily married as her adoptive parents were.

But the woman was shaking her head. She had a sad expression on her face.

"I wish we were," she said. "He was wonderful. But he died in a car accident before we celebrated our first anniversary."

Brenda felt sad for her birth mother and disappointed for herself. Now she could never meet the man who was

such a significant part of her past. She would never know
how he felt about her; she would never know the sound
of his voice.

But, it occurred to her, she could know what he
looked like.

"Do you have any pictures of him?" she asked her
birth mother.

The woman's face brightened.

"Yes, of course!" she said. "I should have thought of
that!"

She walked over to her cluttered buffet, where dozens
of framed photos stood carefully arranged. She picked up
one and brought it back to Brenda.

"Here he is," she said. "I think you have his eyes."

Brenda held the photo in her hands. She took one
look at the handsome face, the wavy, dark hair and the
kind eyes of the man who was smiling out of the frame at
her. And she felt herself go pale.

"Tell me," she said after a moment, when she trusted
her voice again, "what was his name?"

The woman smiled.

"His name was Charles," she said. "But even his parents agreed that the name didn't suit him; it just seemed
too stuffy. So from the time he was a little boy until the
day he died, everyone called him 'Buddy.'"

"I read somewhere that ghosts are the spirits of people who don't realize that they've died. And that made me think, whoa! How do I know I'M not dead? How do you know that YOU'RE not?...

The Dish

Ed Carson hit some more buttons on his huge mother-ship of a remote control. He flipped through the pages of his instruction manual. And he cursed, loudly. He had spent the afternoon installing his brand new satellite dish. The project was not going well and he was beginning to get annoyed.

"Why do these damn things have to be so complicated?" he complained. "Twenty-five pages of bloody instructions and not one of 'em can tell me why the TV's getting such crappy reception."

"I can tell you why," said his wife, Lisa. "It's because you were too cheap to pay for professional installation."

Ed turned to face her. She was lounging on the couch, as usual, flipping through the pages of some glossy fashion magazine. She didn't bother looking up when he spoke to her.

"'Professional installation,' as you put it, cost an extra 200 bucks," he explained. "I know how much you enjoy flushing money down the toilet, but I'm not gonna put out two C-notes to have some trained monkey come over and screw a couple of brackets to the roof. Probably bust a bunch of shingles while he's at it."

Ed did hate to waste money. But what he hated more was watching the way his beautiful, young wife fawned over the brawny types who were typically sent to perform such menial jobs. Some repair guy with big biceps and a tool belt would walk in the door and, suddenly, Lisa was fascinated by the complex workings of the washing machine motor. Normally, Ed couldn't even get her to wash a load of his socks and underwear.

The guys paid plenty of attention to her, too. But, then, anyone with eyes did. She was a knockout, and young, which had seemed to Ed to be a great combination when he talked her into marrying him. A few years later, he was wishing he had taken his brother's advice.

"Get someone your own age," he had told Ed. "Someone with a little less flash. You don't hafta watch 'em so much then, and you don't have to wonder if they married you for your money."

Ed didn't have to wonder. By the time the honeymoon was over, he knew Lisa had married him for his money. And he knew that she had been disappointed to discover that there wasn't more of it.

"You told me you owned those stores!" she had wailed during their first marital row.

"I do," said Ed. "But I've got partners; I've gotta be responsible. We can't just go taking cash out of the business every time you want a new piece of jewelry! And, anyway, I take out a good salary. We got no worries about paying the bills."

She had looked up at him with tearful, big, blue eyes.

"I know, honey," she had said. "But what about—God forbid—if something were to happen…"

"Then you'd own my shares. Plus, I got plenty of insurance," he told her. "So stop worrying! Everything's organized. You're not married to some young fool here."

And it was true. Ed wasn't young. He eventually understood that he was an old fool, married to a beautiful gold digger 23 years his junior.

"Will that thing pick up MTV?" she was saying in a pouty voice.

Ed ignored the question. He was fiddling with the connections on the back of the set.

"Will it pick up *anything?*" Lisa asked.

Ed threw the instruction manual across the room.

"Dammit!" he yelled. "I'm gonna have to get back up on the freakin' roof! I don't believe this!"

Lisa sighed and started to shake a bottle of metallic blue nail polish.

"I hate this," she said. "It sucks having no TV."

"Yeah, that's another real hardship for you," said Ed. "Now get your butt off the couch and come hold the ladder for me."

Lisa glared at him. She held up her left hand, displaying three bright blue fingernails.

"I just started my manicure!" she said.

"So you'll finish it later," he snapped. "Let's go."

🦇

The Carsons owned a big, fancy, two-story house in a prestigious neighborhood of big, fancy, two-story houses. Until today, theirs had been the only one without a

satellite dish trained skyward. Ed looked around and
wondered if any of his neighbors had experienced as
much difficulty getting the thing on line.

"Shouldn't have done this on such a windy day," he
said as he set the extendable aluminum ladder up against
the back wall of the house.

"Duh!" said Lisa, who had plopped herself down on a
patio chair until her services were required. "A professional would have known that."

"I don't need your opinions, I need you to hold the
ladder steady! So get over here!" said Ed.

Lisa rose in a languid manner and strolled as slowly as
she could to where Ed was standing. She steadied the ladder by pressing her palms against it, splaying her fingers
out so her nails would not smudge.

"Pay attention here," said Ed. "I don't need to be
kissin' the patio from 25 feet up."

"Got it," said Lisa. But she sounded entirely uninter-
ested and gazed off into the distance as she spoke.

Ed shook his head in frustration. *I shoulda got a pre-
nup*, he was thinking.

"Okay, steady as she goes" was what he said.

Ed climbed the ladder slowly, yelling at Lisa to hold it
more firmly whenever the wind gusted. By the time he
reached the roof, he was sweating more from fear than
from effort. Ed was in pretty good shape for a man of his
age. But he was more than a little afraid of heights.

"Wait for me, now," he called down to his wife. "I'm
gonna make a couple of adjustments here, and then I'll
need you to go check the TV."

"Sure, whatever," Lisa said. She was back in the patio
chair. She had pulled the bottle of nail polish out of the

pocket of her shorts and was carrying on with her manicure.

Ed crawled over to the place on the roof where he had painstakingly bolted the dish hours earlier. With great care, he altered the tilt of it just a little.

"Lisa!" he yelled, "Go back inside! See if we got reception on this thing!"

With a great sigh, Lisa stood up again and screwed the cap back on her bottle of polish. With electric blue nails held carefully aloft, she wandered across the patio and through the sliding glass doors that led to the recreation room. After a few minutes, she emerged.

"Yeah, it looks good now," she announced.

"Define 'good,'" said Ed.

"'Good' means 'good,'" she said. "You can see the programs now. It doesn't all look like one big snowstorm."

"But how's the definition?" Ed pressed her. "Are there any lines? Is it grainy at all?"

"God, I don't know!" she said. "What do I look like, some geeky TV technician?"

"No!" blasted Ed. "You look like a useless bimbo who can't manage to answer one simple question!"

From two stories above the ground, Ed saw his wife's face twist into a mask of hatred.

"Drop dead!" she shrieked. She stormed off into the rec room, slamming the patio door with such force that the glass nearly shattered. Seconds later, Ed heard the roar of a car engine and the mechanical hum of the automatic garage door as it slowly yawned open. Carefully, he crawled up to the peak of the roof, where he could look over and have a view of the front street. He watched as

Lisa backed her sporty red convertible down the driveway. With tires squealing, she raced off into the distance.

Drop dead. How nice. Ed would realize later—much later, when he was trying to come to grips with what had happened—that those were the last words his wife had spoken to him.

The wind picked up for a solid minute after Lisa left, and Ed flattened himself against the cedar shingles for protection. He imagined that he looked ridiculous up there—spread eagled, his ragged old Bruins t-shirt flapping around him like a flag—but that wasn't what concerned him. What concerned him—heck, what scared him—was that he had to climb back down the ladder without a spotter, seeing as his spotter had gotten herself into the kind of mood that typically required about two dozen roses and 1000 dollars' worth of shoes to cure. Ed looked down at the hard stones of the patio and reminded himself to take more care regarding the timing of future outbursts.

"You can do it," he told himself. "No big deal, just take it slow and easy." He began to inch his way down the roof to the place where he could see the top of the ladder peeking up above the eaves. When he was close enough to touch it, he reached out one hand, took firm hold of one of the side pieces and gave it a shake. The ladder wobbled a little; it was actually more like a slight wave that traveled all the way from the top to the bottom. But the rubber grips at the base remained firmly in position.

"That's good," Ed told himself. "That's solid." Still, he didn't want to take any unnecessary chances. He sat patiently on the edge of the roof, waiting for the wind to calm. When the leaves on the trees stopped fluttering for a few moments, he decided that he had a good window of opportunity. Cautiously, holding his breath, he turned around, extended his leg and placed one foot on the ladder. Then two feet. He moved down a rung at a time until he knew that he would have to let go of the roof if he wanted to descend any farther. Gradually, he loosened his white-knuckle grip, moving first his right hand to the ladder and then his...

A howling blast of wind hit Ed, knocking him sideways and billowing his shirt out like a sail. Before he could center himself, the top of the ladder began to skitter along the roof, making a little *skitch-skitch-skitch* sound as it went. Ed could feel gravity tugging at him. The ladder was dangerously off-balance, and in a second or two his skull was going to smash like an egg against his expensive slate patio.

Ed let go of the ladder. He grabbed desperately at the eaves trough and momentarily caught a sharp metal edge that neatly sliced three of his fingers. But he managed to get an effective grip on it. The wind blew again. The ladder *skitched* again, another jerky movement that put Ed in worse peril. He was so far off center that his body weight was beginning to pull the ladder. He felt himself starting to fall...

In one bold, last-ditch effort, Ed threw himself in the opposite direction of that in which he was falling. He reached out with his bleeding hand and caught firm hold of a decorative shutter that was nailed to the wall outside one of the second-floor windows. The ladder wobbled, but it remained leaning against the house. Then, slowly, very slowly, Ed began to pull it back to center. Once it was there, once it felt relatively stable again, he wasted no time. Without looking down or stopping to think, he descended the ladder as quickly as possible, finally stepping onto the ground with legs that felt as if they were made of water. He collapsed into a patio chair, closed his eyes and sat limply until his heart stopped pounding.

Eventually, Ed opened his eyes and looked up at the top of the ladder. Crimson smears of blood stood out starkly against the shiny aluminum. It was on the shutter, too, and on the eaves trough that had cut him. The sight pleased him in a perverse way.

Let Lisa come home and get a load of that, he thought, and his lips curled into a satisfied little smile. *Let her see what happened because she threw a tantrum.* Then, for the first time, he wondered how badly injured his hand was. Gingerly, he held it up and uncurled his fingers.

But Ed's hand was fine. It hadn't even suffered a scratch.

He was certain it had been his left hand, but he checked his right nevertheless. It, too, was unhurt. He stood up, examining his body. Nothing was cut; nothing was bleeding. But he remembered the pain and the sensation of his skin opening up. And the stains that were on the ladder and the house—they definitely looked like blood and they hadn't been there before. Ed stood for several minutes, looking back and forth between his hand and the dark smears.

"To hell with it," he finally said. It had been a long afternoon of hard work. Lisa had rudely blown him off. He had nearly killed himself coming down the ladder. And he was thirsty. It was time to call it a day and break into the six-pack that he had stashed in the fridge.

Ed's first mission when he got in the house was to grab himself a beer. The second was to check out the television reception. He turned on the set and started flipping through the myriad new channels. Every one of them was coming in crystal clear.

"Finally!" he said. "Now we're talkin'!"

He settled on a sports channel and went into the kitchen to make himself a sandwich. He brought it back into the rec room, along with a second can of beer, so that he wouldn't have to get up when the first one was finished. But he only ended up drinking the one. It seemed flat and tasteless to him, as did the salami-and-cheese sandwich. Ed shrugged it off. He figured that almost dying had probably spoiled his appetite for a few hours.

The satellite TV was wonderful, though. Nothing could spoil that. Ed surfed his new entertainment landscape happily, pausing here and there to catch a few minutes of a familiar movie or a bizarre foreign commercial. He saw the winning goal of a Brazilian soccer match and listened to the commentators jabber away excitedly in Portuguese. And he watched news—endless news programs from locations around the world. Ed discovered that the smaller the center, the more entertainingly cheesy the broadcast tended to be. He found himself glued to a show originating somewhere in the Midwest. It was all hog reports and drought warnings, solemnly delivered by a woman in a horrible madras plaid jacket. At one point, she turned the program over to a jolly-looking weatherman.

"Nice jacket, Susan!" he said with great exuberance.

Ed thought it was better than *Comedy Central*.

At 10 PM, Lisa still had not come home. Ed wasn't surprised. She often stayed with a friend after they fought as a means of punishing him. It was predictable; Ed had come to expect it. If she thought he was going to wait up until all hours worrying, "she had another think coming," as his old man had liked to say. Ed was tired and sore and ready to hit the sack. He treated himself to a long, steamy shower, dropped his soggy towel on the bathroom floor because there was no one around to bitch at him about it and crawled between the sheets.

In the middle of the night, half-asleep, he rose to urinate. Although he was barely conscious, he noticed that there was no longer a heap of wet towel in the middle of the ceramic tile. In the dim light, he felt the place on the wall where his bath towel usually hung. It was still there, still fluffy and dry.

He barely recalled the incident the following morning, and by then it had taken on the blurry, unreal quality of a dream.

Ed slept until nearly noon. He didn't usually stay in bed so late; he hated the disorienting feeling of waking up and having half the day gone. But it was the weekend and he didn't have to work, so he told himself that it didn't really matter.

"It's Sunday," he reminded himself as he pulled on a clean pair of sweatpants. "Nothin' to do but relax." To drive the point home, he walked away without bothering to make the bed.

He could tell right away that Lisa hadn't come home yet. The bed in the guest room was untouched and there was no hint of her perfume in the house. When Ed padded downstairs to fix himself breakfast, he saw that her car keys were still missing from the hook on the wall.

"Spoiled brat," he said aloud as he took a carton of eggs out of the refrigerator. She was waiting for him to call her, waiting for an apology. Then she would want him to beg for her return. Ed cracked three eggs into a frying pan and swore to himself that that wouldn't happen. He stirred them with a fork and thought that it might just be for the best if she stayed gone a good, long time. Then he turned around, meaning to close the egg carton and put it back in the fridge, and what he saw made him stop thinking about Lisa altogether.

There were a full dozen eggs in the carton.

Ed could hear the pan sizzling on the stove behind him. But there were no eggs missing from their little Styrofoam nests. Ed turned around. He saw the broken shells, sitting on the counter in a glistening puddle of egg white. He saw the foamy yellow mixture congealing in the pan. But the carton was still…

Ed turned back to the countertop by the fridge. The egg carton had vanished entirely.

There was a change in the atmosphere, too. The buttery aroma of frying eggs was suddenly gone, as was the appetizing sizzle, and Ed suspected that if he were to look back at the stove he would see nothing but a clean surface. The burners would be neatly hidden by their little toile-patterned covers and there would be no sticky, white shells cluttering the granite counter. So he didn't look at that. Instead, he carefully opened the refrigerator.

The egg carton was back on its shelf, sitting at the precise angle it had been when Ed had first grabbed it out of the fridge.

And there was something else.

He had drunk a beer the night before and he had pulled two beers out of the plastic rings that held the cans together. But the six-pack that sat on the bottom shelf was completely intact. Not one of its frosty soldiers was missing.

Suddenly, Ed felt as if he was swaying dangerously at the top of the ladder again.

"What the hell is this?" he cried. "What's going on?"

But there was no one to answer him. Ed realized at that moment that, despite their differences, he wished Lisa was at home. He needed the reassurance of human company, however crabby it might be. He picked up the phone and dialed his wife's cell number.

He let it ring for a good long time before he was willing to admit that she wasn't going to answer. He swore and hung up and tried to think of where she might be.

Lisa had a friend named Tina who had big hair and an apartment downtown. Ed remembered that she had stayed over there before. He scanned the list of numbers that Lisa kept posted in the kitchen, found Tina's name and dialed. The phone rang 20 times. Neither an answering machine nor a human being picked up. He tried other numbers, numbers that Lisa had neatly written beside names like "Sue" and "Sherry" and "Kim." It seemed that none of them answered their phones on Sunday afternoons.

"Dammit!" Ed yelled, and he threw the cordless phone across the room. Doing it made him feel a little better, a little more in control.

I haven't eaten properly all weekend, he thought. *Blood sugar's low and I'm feeling weird, that's my problem. Gotta get some fuel into the machine.*

But he had no desire to risk cooking again. Instead, Ed grabbed a package of wheat crackers out of the pantry, took them into the rec room and sat down. He opened the box and ate 10 crackers in a row. They had no taste; they seemed to have no substance. When Ed looked into the box, he could see that it was still full to the top. His appetite, the little bit that he had, disappeared at that point.

He decided then that he was just going to sit tight until Lisa got home. She never stayed away for more than a day; she missed her things too much when she was gone. So he would lay low until she returned and then she could get him to a doctor. Ed was certain that a good doctor would be able to find out what the hell was wrong with him.

Just stay put, he decided. *Nobody moves—nobody gets hurt.*

But there was no good reason that he could think of why he shouldn't watch a little TV. Ed picked up the remote and hit the power button. The huge screen came to life. Ed almost laughed when he saw that the program was a rebroadcast of the soccer game he had watched the afternoon before. One of his favorite Springsteen songs came into his head—"57 Channels and Nothin' On." But Ed had in the neighborhood of 200 channels, so he was fairly confident that he could find something worth watching.

There were some movies. Ed had seen them all before; in fact, he remembered seeing bits and pieces of them the day before. There were some sitcom reruns that didn't interest him. And there were endless foreign advertisements, which weren't nearly as amusing once the novelty had worn off. Finally, he happened upon the Midwestern news program that had been so thoroughly entertaining the first time he had seen it. Ed grinned a little in anticipation and put down the remote.

He was only a few minutes in when he discovered that all agricultural reports tended to suffer from a certain sameness. What didn't help was the fact that the news anchor had chosen to wear the ugly madras jacket for a second day running.

Must be her favorite, Ed thought as he watched her introduce Chuckles, The Happy Weatherman. But then he heard the line, "Nice jacket, Susan!" and he froze.

They were rerunning the news? *Nobody* reran the news.

Ed felt as if he was teetering on the top of the ladder again. He closed his eyes until the sensation began to recede. Then he grabbed the remote and shut off the television.

Everything was okay. Everything would be okay. As soon as Lisa got back and took him to the emergency room where they would give him something to take care of the vertigo.

But it was getting late in the afternoon and she still wasn't home. Ed decided to try calling again from the phone in the bedroom. He didn't trust the cordless anymore. He thought it might be broken and that might be the reason he couldn't get through to anyone.

Ed climbed the stairs carefully, holding tight to the railing in case the strange dizziness struck him before he reached the top. But it didn't; he felt fine until he walked into the bedroom and saw that the bed had been neatly made.

Or not slept in at all, said some nasty voice inside his head. Ed chose to ignore the voice. He sat down hard on the plush carpet, took the phone off the nightstand and dialed Lisa's cell.

There was no answer.

Ed tried his work number then. He thought that if he was lucky, one of the guys might be logging a little overtime. But the phone rang endlessly. The machine, with its friendly message regarding hours of operation, did not pick up.

He hung up and tried to think of someone who was sure to be home, someone who would be sure to answer. Just to reassure him that the phone lines were still in operation.

Ed had an idea, then. It was so obvious that he smiled. He picked up the phone, dialed 911 and waited for the comforting sound of an operator's voice.

But the phone just rang and rang.

Ed hung up eventually. He sat on the bedroom floor for a while, listening to the silence of the house. Then, for the first time, he began to wonder where he was instead of where his lovely young wife might be.

Lisa was sitting on a posh sofa, dabbing at her eyes with a tissue, looking fabulous in a sleek, black Versace dress. She hadn't even bothered looking at other designers. It was Lisa's opinion that only Donatella Versace could make a black dress that could say "mournful" and "sexy" at the same time. As for the cost—it didn't concern her. There was insurance money on the way.

"I'm here to help you in any way I can," said the funeral director who sat across from her. His name was Kyle. He was no more than 30, Lisa figured, and totally hot. Even under his somber charcoal suit, she could see that his body was chiseled.

"It's just so hard to deal with," she whispered. "Such a senseless accident. If only he had asked me to hold the ladder…"

She sensed then that it was time for more tears, and she buried her face in her hands, being careful not to smudge her makeup.

"There, there," said Kyle. He moved over to the sofa where Lisa sat in order to comfort her more effectively. "It must be very difficult for you. Of course, if there's anything I can do…"

Lisa sniffled adorably.

"That's sweet," she said. "And you are so easy to talk to. Perhaps you could come over some night, so I could share some things with you?"

"Certainly," said Kyle. "If I can provide a shoulder…"

Lisa brightened.

"Yes," she said, "that would be wonderful." Then she noticed Kyle looking ever so discreetly down the front of her Versace dress and smiled. She knew she could let the grieving widow act lapse a little.

"We could order a pizza or something," she suggested. "Maybe watch some TV. I have a satellite dish," she said as she placed her hand on the funeral director's muscular thigh.

"My mother used to work with this woman who smoked a pack a day, easy. And then, one day, she just totally quit. But she didn't believe in any of that stuff like nicotine gum or patches. She said they didn't work. So my mom kept askin' her how did she quit? And one day this lady says 'I'll tell you if you swear to keep it secret...'"

One Sure Way To Quit

Sharon had left right after work on Friday. Her suitcase had been tucked away in the trunk of her car all day, like a wonderful secret, so she didn't even have to swing by her apartment before heading out of the city. She just locked her office door, negotiated the rush-hour traffic and sailed off down the highway with the stereo blaring and her spirits soaring. It was nearly nine o'clock that night before her mood crashed.

She had pulled into the sleepy little lake resort that was her destination. It was dark—the kind of inky dark that comes in the fall when overcast skies blot out the moon and there's no snow on the ground to reflect the streetlights—and the town was shut tight as a clam. It was the downside of vacationing during the off-season,

Sharon supposed as she slowly cruised the shadowy streets looking for a convenience store.

The one she found was locked up just the same as the other businesses. A hand-lettered "closed" sign hung off-kilter in the front window, just below a scrawl of red neon advertising Sharon's brand of cigarettes. The combination was a particularly mocking one because Sharon, in her haste, had forgotten to pack a week's worth of smokes.

She drummed her fingers on the steering wheel as she considered her options. There was one lonely cigarette remaining in the pack in her purse and she was in desperate need of it at that moment. That would leave her without nicotine until the store opened at nine o'clock Saturday morning. The idea of 12 hours without a cigarette made her consider heading back to the last gas station that she had passed, but that meant at least an hour's worth of driving, round-trip. Sharon stubbornly dismissed the idea. That was the sort of thing that addicts did and, while Sharon was a smoker, she hated to view herself as an addict.

"No big deal," she muttered to herself as she lit the tip of her last cigarette. "I'll come back in the morning."

She blew out a cloud of smoke, took one last resentful look at the "closed" sign and drove away. On the other side of the lake was a bed and breakfast with a room that had her name on it.

It was a smoking room, of course. Sharon had made certain of it. Not that it was necessary, she wasn't that controlled by her habit, but she did want to feel free to do as she liked while on vacation. The first three places she had called had informed her in snooty tones that they were strictly smoke-free. The fourth, Bertie's B & B, was several miles out of town but catered happily to those who still dared to light up in public.

"Sure, you can smoke in the room. You can smoke anywhere in the whole damn place!" the woman on the phone had cackled. "I won't give it up; I can hardly ask my guests to!"

Sharon booked the room with her credit card and spent the next six weeks picturing herself in lovely cable-knit sweaters, surrounded by brilliant fall colors and crisp October air. She imagined lounging in a weathered wooden chair on a creaky dock, reading a good novel while the water lapped at the pilings. She fantasized about a room filled with Victorian clutter and charm and a bed with a duvet that was as snowy and voluminous as a cloud. It was going to be a good holiday, and having a smoking room meant that her relaxation would not be interrupted by any inconvenient cravings.

That had been Sharon's plan, but she was already feeling the urge to light up when she pulled off the main road by the cheerful red and white sign that read "Bertie's B & B! A half mile this way!" By the time she had parked her car in the tidy, gravel roundabout, the urge had taken on the insistent quality of a demand. As Sharon pulled her leather suitcase out of the trunk, she was wishing that she had driven back to the gas station after all.

It's only one night, she thought. *One night can't be that bad.*

But then she walked in the front door of the sprawling old home and changed her mind.

The house was permeated with the smoky aroma of tobacco. Sharon smelled it with the first breath that she

took and saw it in the hazy quality of the yellow light that filled the foyer. Her craving for a cigarette had already kicked into high gear when a stooped, aging woman with wild, steel-wool hair emerged from the parlor with a burning butt gripped between two yellowed fingers.

"Must be Sharon Powell, right?" the woman rasped. "I got no other guests booked right now."

Sharon nodded and set down her suitcase.

"Well, come in then. Come on in. Prob'ly had a long drive, hey? Imagine you want to sit down and relax. You prob'ly figured out I'm Bertie."

Sharon had figured it out, but she didn't care. She was too focused upon the stub of a cigarette that Bertie put to her seamed lips after every little burst of conversation. She was too busy watching the way the tip glowed with every drag.

Her fixation did not go unnoticed.

"Listen," said Bertie, "I can sign ya in later, if you want. Maybe you'd rather have a smoke right about now?"

Sharon found her voice then.

"I'd love to," she admitted, "but I'm all out and the store in town was closed by the time I got there. So I might as well take care of business now because the cigarette will have to wait until morning."

"Like hell!" Bertie cackled. "You may be out, but I'm not! Come on in and sit down and have a visit and a smoke with me!" She shuffled back into the parlor, motioning for Sharon to follow her.

Sharon did follow, feeling stupidly grateful for the promise of a cigarette. *This is how people lure kids into cars with candy,* she thought. But the thought disappeared when Bertie handed over a nearly full pack of smokes and a pink butane lighter. Sharon pulled one out greedily and lit it. Smoke filled her lungs, relief washed over her entire body and, for a terrible moment, she realized just how powerfully hooked she was.

"Oh, thank you," she said as she exhaled and sat down on one of Bertie's rose-colored sofas. "I can't believe I forgot to bring my own."

Bertie chuckled as she lit a fresh cigarette from the butt of her dying one.

"I'd never do that, m'self," she said. "These are my best friends. The kinda friends that get ya in the end, o' course, but still…"

Sharon smiled politely and tapped her ash into the massive blue glass ashtray that dominated Bertie's coffee table. It was filled to overflowing with crushed butts.

They were ugly, pinched at the end and stained yellow with nicotine. None showed the feminine trace of lipstick that branded each of Sharon's cigarettes.

"I intend to quit one of these days," Sharon told her hostess between drags. She was surprised to hear herself saying it even though it was true. It was something that she considered to be nobody else's business. Somehow, that made it even worse when Bertie burst out laughing.

"Oh, don't they all say that!" she howled. "And I suppose it's true, hey? We all quit in the end, honey, don't we?"

Sharon felt herself flush a little.

"There are ways to do it, when a person's ready," she said defensively. "I'm thinking of going to a seminar in the new year. I might even try hypnosis."

Bertie shook her head as she inhaled deeply on her own cigarette.

"That stuff don't work," she said.

Sharon was growing increasingly annoyed.

"It *can*," she insisted. "I'm sure it can, if someone's in the right frame of mind."

Bertie cocked her head thoughtfully. Twin streams of smoke drifted out of her nostrils.

"That what you're waiting for, then?" she asked. "The 'right frame of mind'?"

Sharon was taking quick little puffs on her cigarette, trying to finish it quickly so she could escape to her room.

"I suppose so, yes," she said.

"Well, let me tell ya something," said Bertie. "There's only one sure way to quit, and it's got nuthin' to do with that. It's about being scared—good an' scared."

"Well, anyone who reads the warnings has reason to worry…"

"Not like that," Bertie cut Sharon off abruptly. "I'm not talking about niggling little fears. I'm talking about a big, bad scare. The kind that snaps you back. Like a bad chest X-ray or havin' the doc outfit you with one of those little portable oxygen units. Or watching someone die of a heart attack right in front of you while you're lined up to buy your morning coffee. That kind of scare. Anyone I've ever known who's given up the habit has had a good scare like that."

Sharon stubbed out her cigarette then, even though there was a good inch of it left.

"If you don't mind, I'm going to turn in," she said. "It's been a long day."

"I hope you get scared," Bertie continued as if she hadn't heard Sharon, "because these things'll kill ya, otherwise. That's a fact. That's a for-sure fact."

Sharon produced another tight little smile and stood up.

"Shall I sign in now and get my room key?" she asked.

Bertie squinted at her through the blue haze.

"Oh, sure," she said. "'course, you're welcome to visit some more and have another smoke if you like."

Sharon might have laughed had she been less tired and ragged around the edges.

"Thanks," she said instead. "I'll pass."

Bertie shrugged as if to say *your loss, lots of good smokes and good conversation down here, but if you're bound and determined…*She pushed herself out of her seat and shuffled back out into the foyer to the little oak desk where Sharon had left her suitcase. She asked

Sharon a couple of questions, took an imprint of her credit card and handed over a key that was attached to a paddle-sized gold tag.

"Down the back hall, on your right," she directed. "Got a view of the lake, out that window. Not that you can see it proper in the dark."

"I'll enjoy it tomorrow," Sharon said as she collected her suitcase and walked away. Before she was around the corner, her nostril picked up the sharp scent of Bertie lighting another cigarette, probably from the smoldering butt of her last one.

The room was pretty enough, but it was hot and it stank of cigarettes. Sharon's eyes were beginning to feel watery and bloodshot from the smoky haze that filled every inch of the house.

She never airs it out, that's why it's so bad, she thought, and she tried to open her window. The latch was jammed though, and Sharon thought it better to give up rather than to ask Bertie for assistance and risk hearing more of her grim advice. Instead, she put on the lightest night-gown she had brought, threw the reeking, puffy quilt off the bed and slid in between the smoky-smelling sheets. The stench disgusted her, but still her last thought before falling asleep was a wish for her customary bedtime cigarette.

In her nightmare, Sharon was being roasted in a huge oven while Bertie peered through the little window, as if to check on her progress. The old woman nodded approvingly at the way Sharon's skin was turning crisp and black. Sharon tried to call out for help, but when she parted her lips, a blast of scorching wind invaded her throat, fusing her vocal chords. Bertie seemed to chuckle at this and shook her head as if to say *Ain't that just always the way it goes?* Then she held her cigarette up to the glass where Sharon could see it and mouthed the words *Only one sure way to quit.*

"A good scare, a real good scare," Sharon found herself mumbling repeatedly as she clawed her way back to consciousness. Eventually, as she realized that she had been dreaming, she grew quiet. She kicked off the top sheet, searching for some relief from the heat that had induced the nightmare. Her nightgown was pasted against her skin with perspiration and her eyes felt hot and dry. She reached for the glass of water that she had left on the nightstand and took a sip. She spat it out immediately and switched on the bedside lamp.

Gray flakes of ash had settled on the surface of the water. Several curls of it were swirling lazily on their way to the bottom of the glass.

By morning, Sharon understood that the ashes in the water had simply been another part of the dream. She had thrown the evidence down the sink in a fit of disgust at the time, but still she was sure. What was more important was the fact that it didn't matter. The sun was shining and she was about to drive into town for a carton of lovely cigarettes. Then she would come back to Bertie's, collect her suitcase and check herself out. A nice, fresh, comfortable room at an establishment where the innkeepers were known for not handing out unsolicited advice was where she wanted to spend the remainder of the week.

She tiptoed down the hall and across the foyer, trying to ignore the heavy smell of frying grease and burnt toast. Bertie was probably shuffling around the kitchen, cooking with a cigarette dangling from her thin, dry lips. Sharon felt a little guilty, skipping out without a word, but she desperately needed some air. And she needed to have her morning cigarette—or maybe two or three—before she felt capable of dealing with the old woman and her sackful of morbid wisdom.

The screen door had a creak to it, and Sharon held her breath as she slipped out onto the front porch. She skipped lightly down the three broad, wooden steps and then could not stop herself from running around to the driver's side door of her car. She was shaking as she fumbled with her keys, trying to grasp the one that unlocked the door. *This is where they always get you,* was her panicked thought. *Just when you're so close to being safe, nearly home free...*

The key turned neatly in the lock. Sharon pulled the door handle with such force she tore a fingernail down to the quick. But she didn't stop to examine it. She jumped into the car, slammed and locked the door and fired the ignition. Then she threw the car into gear and pressed her foot into the gas pedal. The tires sent out a shower of gravel as she pulled away, but Sharon didn't so much as glance into the rearview mirror. She had a horrible fear that she would see Bertie there, standing on the porch, waving her back.

Come on in, now, I got a pot of coffee and a pack of smokes waiting for ya. Light up, there ya go, I'll tell ya some more about how these things'll kill ya in the end.

It was ridiculous, of course; Sharon had given herself a shot of adrenaline by playing her little game of Let's Sneak Out and Not Get Caught. It was all in her imagination. Still, she avoided looking back and didn't crack the window for a breath of fresh air until she had turned onto the main road.

Someone inside the store was turning the sign around to read "open" just as Sharon pulled up to the front.

"Mornin'," said a middle-aged man in a western-style shirt when she walked in the door. "Looks like it's gonna be a pretty day, hey?"

Sharon smiled and nodded but made no effort at casual conversation.

"Cigarettes," she said. "And coffee. Fast as possible, please." She started pulling bills out of her wallet and laying them on the counter by the cash register. The storekeeper chuckled as though Sharon had told him a joke but moved along smartly to serve her just the same.

Five minutes later, she was feeling *so* much better. She was on her second cigarette by then and was enjoying luxurious long drags of smoke in between luxurious long swallows of extra sweet coffee. There were no other customers, and it wasn't long before the storekeeper wandered outside to the leaning picnic table where Sharon was enjoying her morning ritual.

"You holidaying, or passin' through?" he inquired.

"I'm here for a week," Sharon replied. "Little bit of a vacation."

The man nodded. He planted his hands on his hips and stretched his torso to the left and then the right. The western shirt pulled tight across his paunchy belly. Its mother-of-pearl snaps threatened to pop.

"You're smart to come in the off-season," he said. "No crowds, and the weather can be fine. Cheaper to book a room, too. And easier."

"I'm thinking of changing accommodations," Sharon said, then. "I don't suppose you know of anyplace that hasn't declared smoking the evil of all evils?"

The man knit his brow as he stared off into the distance.

"There's one or two," he finally said. "I can write 'em down for you. Used to be more, but the "Whispering Pines" there, it just went smoke-free, and another place burned down last month."

"Really?" Sharon said, although she was less than interested in the storekeeper's account of last month's news.

"Yep," he said. "A nice bed and breakfast on the far side of the lake. Started with a cigarette—that's what the fire chief says, anyhow. There were no guests in the place, which was a lucky thing, but the lady who owned the place died. Name was Bertie Cooper. Real nice lady. Good customer of mine."

"Not Bertie's B & B?" Sharon said. She knew that it couldn't be, yet still she felt her stomach shift uncomfortably. Her hand became a little unsteady and she set her Styrofoam cup down on the splintered surface of the table.

The storekeeper didn't notice her sudden tension. He was staring down the road looking for his next potential customer as he answered.

"The very one," he said, sadly. "The very one."

She must have misunderstood.

Sharon kept telling herself that as she drove along the narrow, winding road that led her around the lake. It was the only explanation. After a bad evening and a bad sleep, she had misheard words, creating a reflection of her nervous, paranoid, mental state. It was a bit like the way she often misread news headlines at first glance, so that they told her more about what was on her mind than what was in the paper. She was experiencing a similar sort of confusion over what the storekeeper had told her. It was the only logical explanation.

Being armed with a logical explanation didn't keep the gooseflesh from rising up on her arms when she turned down the drive at the corner with the cheerful billboard, however. It didn't keep an icy stone from settling in the pit of her stomach as she approached the turn where she would emerge from the trees and Bertie's Bed & Breakfast, with its neat gravel roundabout, would come into full view. It didn't stop her from thinking that she could still go back—what was she abandoning after all? Just a suitcase, just some clothing and toiletries that could be easily replaced.

But there was more than a suitcase full of holiday essentials at stake. Sharon had to know. She needed proof that her problems were no greater than questionable hearing, a wild imagination and a guilt complex about her butt habit. She required assurance that the world was still functioning under the same basic laws of what was and was not possible.

Once she turned the last corner, however, she knew that simply wasn't true.

The circular gravel driveway was still there. Beyond it, 100 yards or so down the bank, Sharon could see the lake. But, between the two, where Bertie's B & B should have stood, there was nothing but a charred ruin.

Blackened timbers leaned upon one another like fallen logs, forming an awkward, scorched teepee over the field of ashy debris. A few skeletal remains of items that hadn't been completely incinerated poked defiantly out of the rubble. There was a stove and a refrigerator still standing in the part of the house where Sharon had smelled the grease and burning toast only an hour earlier. There was the sooty, twisted frame of the screen door that had creaked so loudly as she left the house.

"This is impossible," Sharon whispered as she opened the door of her car and stepped out. "This can't be."

She could almost feel the mechanics of her mind at that point. She sensed her defensive mechanisms scrambling to find some way of denying it all while her memory ground away, calling up the overpowering stench of smoke and the oppressive heat that she had suffered through the night. Her imagination kicked in on top of the other mental functions then, telling her that the experience was like a vapor; it was a ghost of what had happened at the location weeks before her arrival.

Then she saw her suitcase, and any chance that she might have had at denial was destroyed. It was sitting on the far side of the debris field in a spot where a person might have once been able to look out a window and enjoy a nice view of the lake.

Sharon picked her way carefully through the sooty remains and collected her camel-colored leather bag. It stood out like a smooth, pale scar on a grimy face; it was the only thing in the vicinity that had not been singed, melted or reduced to crumbling charcoal. At least she *thought* it was the only thing. But, as Sharon stepped cautiously through the black ruin, she spotted something else.

It was the enormous blue glass ashtray, the one that had sat between her and Bertie the night before. Its deep aquamarine color was nearly obscured with dark smears of ash, and it had come to sit on the foundation, atop a heap of debris that must have been what remained of the coffee table. Sharon remembered it being piled high with butts, but only one was left. A fresh, white one. One with a good inch of cigarette remaining and a little telltale ring of copper-colored lipstick on the filter. Sharon stared at it, and she remembered what Bertie had told her as she was crushing it out.

I hope you get scared, because these things'll kill ya, otherwise. That's a for-sure fact.

Sharon truly understood then. It *was* a for-sure fact for Bertie, who had been cremated in her bed because of one smoldering coffin nail that had fallen behind the drapes or made a fiery home for itself between the dry kindling of two blankets. The whole horror of it took root in Sharon's mind then, and she stopped picking a cautious path through the rubble. Instead, she ran— across the torched wreckage, around the gravel roundabout, all the way to her car, where she stuffed her suitcase into the front seat like some bulky, tan passenger and fired the ignition. Then, before she put the transmission into gear, she pulled a long, white box out of the space between the bucket seats and heaved it out the window. It was the carton of cigarettes that she had purchased not one hour earlier.

"These are for you, Bertie!" she screamed. "I'm giving it up!"

Sharon drove away, knowing that she'd never light another smoke.

She'd been scared. Plenty scared. And she had heard that was the one sure way to quit.

The Halloween Party
—The End

"…and she never, ever lit another smoke. At least, that's what my mom tells me."

The second-floor study in Slater Manor remained filled with teens—they sat on the sofas and the tables and the floor and anywhere else they could claim a semi-comfortable perch. But, despite the size of the group, they made no noise. Sounds of the continuing party drifted up from the rooms below, but every person sitting in the story circle was silently respectful of the person who was telling the tale. Even Claire, tucked into the cushioned window seat beside her new friend, Charles, had been unexpectedly drawn into the atmosphere.

But there was a lull. Countless stories had been told; perhaps they were all the stories meant to be shared on that particular Halloween. When it became obvious that no one else was about to tell a tale, people gradually began to discuss the things that they had heard.

"Man, Adam, that story about the guy and the elevator—that freaked me out."

"I've still got goose bumps from that one about the phone calls from the cemetery."

"Haunted house stories are the creepiest. Could you imagine *living* in a haunted house?"

"This house is haunted." Claire was surprised by the sound of her own voice. She felt herself flush a little when the room grew quiet again and all eyes turned to her.

"Well, I mean, I don't know that for sure," she stammered as she fixed her eyes on her shoes, "but I do know that something totally weird happened here once."

Claire kept her gaze downcast but could feel the group staring at her. She was wishing fervently that she had said nothing, when Charles spoke.

"Tell them," he encouraged her gently. "Everyone's waiting. I'm waiting."

It occurred to Claire that it would be easy enough to make some excuse about why she didn't want to tell the story. She could say that she didn't really know the details. Or that it wasn't her story to tell. But the truth was that she remembered every single detail and it was her story to tell; she alone had owned it in the two years since her grandfather had died. Claire was the only one who knew the story, and she knew that there would never be a more appropriate time to share it. She took a deep breath and looked around the room. All eyes were upon her. It seemed as though the group really did want to hear her story.

"When my grandpa was like—I don't know—14 or 15," she hesitantly began, "he used to work in this house. He did odd jobs for Mr. Slater, the guy who built this place. Grandpa used to rake up leaves or weed the garden or polish silver. Whatever. Mrs. Slater was already dead then, so Grandpa figured that there were times Mr. Slater wanted him around for the company as much as anything else.

"There was a kid, I guess, a son—but he was off fighting in Europe. This was during the Second World War. Grandpa said that Mr. Slater was always telling him that his boy had been in this battle or that invasion or he was getting a medal for something or other. Totally proud, you know? So when the war ended and he found out that his son was coming home, he just about exploded with excitement. He was all 'oh, we've got to fix up the attic apartment—everything has to be ready and perfect!' He got my grandpa to do all this work up there. But then Slater's son got home, and nothing was really like the old man expected.

"I guess this guy wasn't at all interested in talking about all the glorious battles he'd been in. Grandpa said he was just—I don't know—fragile. Totally shell-shocked or something. Who knows what he'd seen? But I guess he had nightmares all the time. Even during the day, he'd kind of space out now and then. He couldn't concentrate very well on a conversation. And Grandpa said he'd come over sometimes, he'd be doing some chore, and upstairs, in the attic apartment, he could hear this guy just crying and crying. Old Mr. Slater, he didn't know what to do about it, so he kind of ignored the whole situation. And then, eventually, the son was so absolutely tormented that he went up to his room in the attic one night, pulled out his service revolver and shot himself in the head.

"I guess that at the funeral, the old man looked as though he had aged 20 years. Afterward, when everybody was having coffee and sandwiches, he made a point of coming over to my grandpa. He asked him if he could drop by the house the next day, because he had an important job for him to do. So Grandpa said 'sure.' I mean, what could he say, right?

"So the next day came, and Grandpa came by. And get this: Mr. Slater asked my grandpa, who was just, like, a *kid* at the time, to go upstairs and clean the bloodstain off the floor. He told him 'I can't do it, but I can't stand to think of it there, either. It's keeping me up at night.' So Grandpa got a bucket of water and a bar of soap and a scrub brush and he went up there. He told me that it took him hours. He scrubbed until his back ached and his fingers were just raw. It was, like, the only thing that he could do to help the old man, and he wanted to do something. So he really put his back into it and got the floor totally gleaming. He said that you couldn't tell where the body had been found. Which was why he was pretty surprised by Slater's reaction when he came back to work the next day.

"He said that the minute he was in the door, the old man lit into him about slacking off and not doing his job. And my grandpa was, like, 'what?!' So he went up to the attic to check it out.

"And the bloodstain was still there.

"He was stunned, you know. It made no sense whatso- ever. But he just did the only thing that he could think of and that was to get out the bucket and brush and clean it up all over again. He said that he just did it—he didn't let himself think about it too much. But he made sure that he was here at the house extra early the next day, so he could check the floor before Mr. Slater got a chance to. Just as a precaution, you know. He didn't really think that the stain would still be there.

"But it was.

"It was there, just this big, dark, gory-looking stain, like no one had ever touched it. So my grandpa panics, knowing that Slater could be checking on him at any minute. He grabs a rag and some water out of a wash basin and just starts scrubbing at the edge of this thing. He had only managed to get a little patch of the floor cleaned when he happened to glance back to the place where he started rubbing. And that's when he saw it.

"The stain was reforming itself, behind him.

"So he totally freaked. He went tearing down the stairs and started blithering to Mr. Slater about what was going on and how he wasn't going back up there, ever—not for any amount of money. Slater just looked at him like he was crazy, I guess. Grandpa said he had this hard look about him and he didn't say anything. He just turned on his heel and went up to the attic by himself. But 10 minutes later, when he came down, I guess he was as pale as milk. He goes to Grandpa, 'Frank, get me some planks from the shed.' So Grandpa did. Then, together, they barred the door closed. The one in the back hall.

"Mr. Slater lived alone here for a long time after that. He died in something like 1975 or '76, and someone bought this house at an estate sale. And Grandpa knew this guy—this contractor or something—who was brought in to do some renovations. And he heard that when they ripped off those bars and opened up the door to the attic, something happened. I don't know what. He either didn't know or didn't want to tell me, but something kept them from going up those attic stairs. I guess the people that bought the house called off the renovation and never even moved in.

"For the next 20 years or so, the property kind of passed from one person to another. Mostly, it was rented out—but nobody ever lived here very long. It sat empty a lot. And I heard that anyone who ever went up those stairs just ended up bolting the door shut again. I don't know why for sure. But I used to have some bad dreams about what people saw up there. And I always thought that it was sad, you know. About the son. Anyway, that's my story."

Claire hugged herself protectively and waited for the deadening silence to end. She was expecting ridicule, in some fashion, but it never came.

"God, I bet the ghost of Slater's son is what's up there," one girl breathed. "Can you imagine?" She shifted her eyes toward the ceiling.

"It might be the old man who's haunting the place," someone else offered.

"Well, that's if it really is haunted," Claire said. "I'm just telling you what I was told. I mean, it's impossible to know for sure…"

But no one was hearing her disclaimer. They were too caught up in the tale and the delicious possibility that it was true.

"What about the bloodstain?" someone wondered. "Do you suppose it's still there?"

"Oh, it's still there," came a voice that startled Claire a little. It was Charles, who had been so silent and so still that she had nearly forgotten about him in the course of telling her story.

"How do you know?" someone asked.

Claire expected Charles to tell the group that he had once lived in the house, that he knew its every nook, cranny and oddity because of the time he had spent in it, but he didn't. Instead, he furrowed his brow and blinked several times as if fighting off a persistent headache. Then, when he did speak, he looked very much as if his answer was a surprise, even to him.

"Why—because it's my blood," was what he said.

It seemed to Claire to be such a typically adolescent sort of joke that she was disappointed at first. But when she turned to fix Charles with a disgusted look, she saw that he wasn't laughing or even smiling. In fact, his face seemed suddenly drained of expression. Slumped against the side of the window seat, he seemed as pale and insubstantial as the moonlight that washed over him.

"What's the matter?" Claire said.

Charles didn't respond. He didn't turn to Claire or even appear to hear her question. He continued to stare straight ahead, as though in a trance, as he pushed himself away from the wall, lifted his chin and squared back his shoulders. Then he rose to his feet and began walking across the room.

"Your blood—good one, man," someone snickered as he strode past. But Charles didn't stop and he didn't comment in return. He simply kept walking, eyes ahead, arms at his side, until he reached the door. Then he opened it—one boy who was sitting closest to the doorway later thought that it had seemed to be an impossibly small opening—and he quietly left.

Claire didn't see Charles leave. She hadn't even spared him a glance as he was crossing the room in his strange, robotic fashion. From the moment he had stood up, her eyes had been fixed on a certain spot on the wall inside the window nook. There, spoiling the yellowed floral wallpaper, was a dark, dripping, baseball-sized stain. Its center lay exactly where Charles had been resting his temple.

"Where'd your friend go?" someone asked her. The question, spoken just inches from her face, was enough to shake Claire from her shocked state.

"What?" she asked, stupidly.

"Your friend. That guy. Where'd he take off to?" A petite, friendly girl whom Claire knew from study hall was standing beside her. "Do you think he'd mind if I sat here?" she asked as she rubbed her backside. "The floor's getting a little hard."

Claire was too horrified to speak. Instead, she gestured mutely at the bloody mess, which had by then run all the way down the wall to the cushions of the window seat. A dark, spongy, sinister shape had begun to spread there.

But the girl took Claire's gesture to be an invitation.

"Oh, thanks," she sighed. "This is great."

The girl looked directly at the blood. She sat on the wet patch of the cushion. And she showed no reaction; there was no revulsion in her eyes whatsoever.

Suddenly, Claire was shaking. There were pillows pressed against her ears and a buzzing in her head and the events of the evening seemed dreamy and distant. She didn't understand what had happened. She felt that she would never understand.

Unless she saw him again.

Claire stood up and ran. She ran across the room, dodging furniture and leaping over the people sitting on the floor with their legs stretched out leisurely before them. She banged her thigh hard against the corner of an

antique curio table and nearly fell flat out when she tripped on the corner of a shabby Oriental rug. But nothing stopped her. She crossed the crowded room in record time, pulled open the door and charged out into the hall.

It was much more crowded than it had been before. People who had grown tired of dancing and shouting had migrated upstairs where they could talk to one another and stand a chance of being heard. They crowded the hall, spoiling Claire's view. She desperately looked this way and that, peeking in between bodies and craning her neck to see over heads. Finally, in frustration,

she decided to simply follow her instincts. She made her
way toward the broad staircase and was rewarded with a
rush of relief when she glimpsed a bit of khaki material
somewhere near the landing.

"Charles!" she shouted, but her voice was useless
against the din of the party. Claire squeezed past a raucous group of jocks who were blocking the stairs and
began to make her way down. She clutched the railing to
keep from being pushed down as she descended through
the crowd. She continued to scan for Charles but didn't
see him again until she had reached the bottom.

He was striding toward the back hall by that time,
gliding in a nearly effortless way that mocked Claire's
struggle to move through the mob.

"Stop that guy!" she yelled, hoping that someone
might help her. "Someone grab that soldier guy!"

But no one did. The odd person turned to look in the
direction of her frantic gaze, but then they would shrug
and go back to whatever they had been doing. Mean-
while, Claire could see Charles' broad, khaki shoulders
and dark hair growing ever more distant.

He turned the corner into the shadowy back hall a full
minute before she was able to. She was certain that she
had lost him at that point. But when she emerged from
the wall of partyers who were packed as tightly as sar-
dines but, for some reason, resisted moving into the cool,
spacious hall, there Charles was.

He seemed to be waiting for her. He was standing just
off to the side of the boarded-up door, his hand resting
lightly in the air where a doorknob would have been had
there been one. The vacant look had left his eyes; Claire
felt him looking at her and not through her.

"Are you all right?" she said as she tried to catch her breath.

Charles smiled to show her that he was.

"Thank you," he said. "I understand now. I can go."

Claire didn't want him to leave, and she tried to move toward him. But Charles simply held up one hand—in either a wave or a gesture meant to ward her off—and then, suddenly, he was gone.

"Charles?" she whispered, but there was no response. The Halloween party thumped wildly only a few yards away, but the back hall seemed suspended in a bubble of cool air and silence.

Slowly, as if in a dream, Claire approached the heavy, barred door. She reached out one hand to touch it. Then she heard the almost imperceptible, low, static hum and felt the small, fine hairs on her arms twitching attentively. She withdrew her hand quickly, turned on her heel and left the back hall without giving the door so much as another look.

Claire found Kate still socializing in the upstairs study.

"I have to go home," Claire told her simply. "I feel sick."

Someone of a less forgiving nature might have told Claire to find her own way. But Kate took one look at her friend's pale, drawn face and immediately forgot her earlier rudeness. She picked up an empty potato chip bag and pressed it into Claire's hands.

"In case you have to barf in the car," she said as she began to lead Claire away. Claire allowed herself to be led, only pausing once at the door to look across the room at the cushioned window seat where she and Charles had been.

There was no bloodstain on the wall.

The lane that had felt so ominous on the way to the party seemed blessedly cool and quiet on the way out. The girls drank in the fresh air and walked side by side, Claire silent and broody, Kate full of gossipy chat about the party.

As they were approaching the looming iron gates, Claire grabbed Kate's arm and stopped suddenly.

"Wait a minute," she said. "Can I have your keys?"

"If you're sick, I don't think you should drive."

"No, no, I don't want to drive," said Claire, suddenly animated. "I want that little flashlight on your key chain."

Kate handed over the key chain with its tiny penlight. Claire grabbed it eagerly, switched it on and walked into the overgrown garden.

"You should have peed before you left the house!" Kate called after her. Claire said nothing. She was too busy pulling handfuls of dead vines out of her path.

It took only a few minutes for Claire to find what she was looking for: a somber row of moldering little marble statues. Using the penlight's tiny, focused beam, she scanned the monuments, looking for something, some information. She wasn't sure exactly what it would be.

Each sculpture was different—chosen, presumably, to reflect the person whom it memorialized. Claire paused only briefly over the likenesses of a sorrowful woman in flowing robes, a tiny lamb and a pair of stone hands holding an open bible. She stopped when she came to a soldier.

She nearly shredded the skirt of her dress wiping away the years of grime from the flat nameplate that sat just below the soldier's boots. Eventually, though, Claire was able to read the simple inscription that was there. *C. Slater*, it read. *A hero, 1923–1946.*

"C." *As in Charles,* Claire thought, and automatically she looked up at the lonely turret window that was just visible above the treetops. At first glance she was certain she saw a dim light there and a silhouette against it. But in the blink of an eye it was gone. Claire realized at that moment that she was bone-tired, shivering and that someone was calling her.

"Are you *coming?*" Kate was shouting. "Because I'm *freezing* out here! I'm not exactly dressed for the weather, you know!"

"I'm coming…" Claire called back. To herself she muttered, "I'm totally losing it."

Then, suddenly, there was a quiet, insistent voice in her head.

There's more to this world than we know, said the voice. It was Charles, speaking to her as he had in the study as they sat by the window overlooking the tangled garden. By the time Claire had found her way back to the wonky cobblestone path, she had decided that she might as well believe him.

Once the hatchback's heater kicked in, Kate was back to her cheery self. She began busily babbling to Claire, trying to draw her out.

"Are you feeling better? Because you look better," she announced. "You probably just needed a little air. There were, like, *hundreds* of people crammed in there. I mean—*huge* house, but still. Derek got completely overzealous with the guest list, hey? Either that or else everyone who was invited brought 10 close friends."

Claire "hmm'd" in response. She was gazing out the window, counting the jack-o'-lanterns that had gone dark. The trick-or-treaters were all home in bed, she supposed. There was little reason to keep the candles burning.

"I said 'Did you have a good time at least?'" Kate asked for what must have been the second time.

"It was interesting," nodded Claire.

"'Interesting,'" Kate repeated. "Well, okay, I guess that's better than 'boring.' And how 'bout that guy?" she probed. "Do you think you're going to see that guy again?"

Claire felt a chill settle in the pit of her stomach.

"I seriously doubt it," she told Kate.

Kate shrugged. She knew there was no point in pushing Claire when she wasn't interested in a boy.

"Okay. Well, at least you didn't stay home by yourself and eat a pound of candy corn in front of a *Munsters* rerun."

There was truth in that; Claire knew that it was exactly what she would have done had she been left to her own devices. Suddenly, she saw how horrid and moody and ungrateful she was being in the face of Kate's endless good cheer.

"Listen, Kate," she said, sincerely, "I want to apologize for—you know, for before. And for everything. And thanks for dragging me out tonight."

"Oh, sure." Kate shrugged it off in her breezy way.

"No, I mean it. If I hadn't gone to that party, I would have had such a lame, ordinary Halloween. And I would have missed my last chance ever to see—the inside of that old house. Some day I just would have driven by and seen a big ugly block of new condos and I never would have known that I'd missed something so—special. So thank you."

Kate smiled warmly at her. She had never been the type to hold a grudge.

"Any time," she said as she pulled up in front of Claire's house.

Claire climbed out of the car and was halfway up her own front sidewalk when Kate called out to her.

"Hey!"

Claire turned around. Kate had rolled down the window and was anxiously waving at her.

"I never told you," she said with a grin. "I liked your story."

Claire smiled back and nodded her appreciation.

"Thanks," she said. She paused before adding, "I'll tell you another one sometime. When I'm ready."

Then she turned back and walked up the steps of her front porch, where a stubby remnant of wax was still burning inside her own carefully carved pumpkin. She used the key under the mat to open the door and, as she was replacing it, leaned over and blew out the jack-o'-lantern's stubborn flame.

Halloween, with all its stories and mysteries, was over for another year.

ENJOY MORE SPOOK-TACULAR TALES IN THESE COLLECTIONS FROM GHOST HOUSE BOOKS

GHOST STORIES OF CHRISTMAS *by Jo-Anne Christensen*
This collection of dramatically recreated stories shows that even ghosts have a weakness for the magic of Christmas. Journey with snowbound travelers through the Rocky Mountains, and warm yourself by the woodstove in a simple log home on the prairies. Celebrate the holidays with tales of generosity and fellowship from across North America. These Christmas ghost stories capture the true "spirits" of the season.
$10.95US/$14.95CDN • ISBN 1-55105-334-9 • 5.25" x 8.25" • 224 pages

HAUNTED CHRISTMAS GHOST STORIES *by Jo-Anne Christensen*
Haunted Christmas continues the tradition of sharing captivating and heart-warming tales of ghosts and angels during a magical time of year. Gather round and enjoy these enchanting read-aloud stories.
$10.95US/$14.95CDN • ISBN 1-894877-15-2 • 5.25" x 8.25" • 208 pages

CAMPFIRE GHOST STORIES *by Jo-Anne Christensen*
Read-aloud stories perfect for the late evening hours around a campfire in the woods.
$10.95US/$14.95CDN • ISBN 1-894877-02-0 • 5.25" x 8.25" • 224 pages

GHOSTS, WEREWOLVES, WITCHES AND VAMPIRES *by Jo-Anne Christensen*
A collection of riveting short stories about four of the best-known creatures in paranormal mythology. Although the accounts are dramatized, each is based on events believed to be true. Above all, they're fun to read, full of memorable characters.
$11.95US/$14.95CDN • ISBN 1-55105-333-0 • 5.25" x 8.25" • 224 pages

HAUNTED HOTELS *by Jo-Anne Christensen*
Christensen has put together another spooky collection of tales of the unexplained—this time about the uninvited guests that haunt the hotels of North America and Great Britain. Take this guided tour of 36 haunted hotels.
$10.95US/$14.95CDN • ISBN 1-894877-03-9 • 5.25" x 8.25" • 232 pages

HAUNTED THEATERS *by Barbara Smith*
Some personalities simply won't accept that final curtain call. Best-selling ghost stories author Barbara Smith has conjured up an entertaining collection of tales about spirits and unexplained phenomena that sometimes steal the spotlight in North America's theaters.
$10.95US/$14.95CDN • ISBN 1-894877-04-7 • 5.25" x 8.25" • 224 pages

These and many more Ghost House books are available from your local bookseller or by ordering direct. U.S. readers call 1-800-518-3541.
In Canada, call 1-800-661-9017.